D0997765

CLIMAX

There isn't much to the town of Climax: just another dusty, wind-blown community biding its time until the desert reclaims it. Then its council decides that maintaining a marshal is an unnecessary expenditure. With the town having dispensed with his services, ex-Marshal Frost is let go to make his way out onto the desert — but that is the signal the gathering outlaw gang has been waiting for. They want Climax, and mean to make it their hideout: an outlaw town where they rule the roost . . .

C. J. SOMMERS

CLIMAX

Complete and Unabridged

LINFORD
Leicester

First published in Great Britain in 2013 by
Robert Hale Limited
London

First Linford Edition
published 2015
by arrangement with
Robert Hale Limited
London

A catalogue record for this book is available
from the British Library.

ISBN 978–1–4448–2359–2

Published by
F. A. Thorpe (Publishing)
Anstey, Leicestershire

Set by Words & Graphics Ltd.
Anstey, Leicestershire
Printed and bound in Great Britain by
T. J. International Ltd., Padstow, Cornwall

This book is printed on acid-free paper

1

Climax was the name of the dog-tired pretense of a village which lay in the afternoon shadows of the San Jacinto Mountains, east of the good timber country, west of the rich grasslands. No one remembered how the town had gotten its name. Speculation only concluded that whoever had named it must have been a very desperate and lonesome sort of man.

The rutted main street of Climax sprouted weeds along its length — greasewood and other hardy plants predominating along the edges of the thoroughfare where the passing ponies could not easily trample them down. The truth was not many ponies passed along the street. A dog lying in the middle of the road was in little danger of being disturbed.

For schooling the kids of Climax

played marbles in the dusty alleyways, rolled hoops down Main Street and sat outside the Alhambra Saloon, learning how to cuss from the men inside. The men inside the dark, over-warm saloon profited as much, drinking whatever whiskey and beer they could afford at the moment, playing loud games of poker or losing their money on the spinning numbers on the Alhambra's warped roulette wheel. Everyone knew the wheel was crooked — not rigged, but certainly it did not spin true, but no matter — when a man feels compelled to lose his money he'll take any available game to do it.

A few of the old-timers had figured the wheel out, but these never had much money, having lost it all in the days before they figured it. No one complained. Where was Charles Toledo, the Alhambra's owner, to be expected to get another wheel? Even if one were available, Toledo, of course, would have been disinclined to purchase it. This one had paid him off so well over the years.

Now and then a stranger would ride his horse at a walk past Marshal Giles Frost's office, shake his head and continue on his way. That was a source of enjoyment for the local dogs and kids who would call at the stranger and pursue the wanderer far out of town, sometimes throwing rocks at his horse to hurry it on its way. Once one of two-day-a-week stagecoaches had passed through town with a woman on board. The saloon had emptied out with all the men clamoring for position, gaping at the remarkable sight. They talked about the grand event for months afterward.

For the most part the excitement in Climax came from watching two dogs fighting in the middle of the street, or the occasional fist fight in the Alhambra, usually instigated by sheer boredom. For the most part the Alhambra did nothing more than sit and bake in the desert sun, slowly if imperceptibly fading from the world's memory. Four of the twelve buildings along Main Street were faced with peeling white paint. It baked, flecked and peeled away from all the south-facing façades. The kids liked to peel of the larger flakes and sail them on the breeze. The rest of the town was raw, sun-grayed wood. People had learned that it was no use trying to apply paint.

Besides, by the time they were built, Climax's lone store had run out of house paint years ago.

This was the realm that Giles Frost was paid by the town to protect from lawlessness.

He was allowed free meals at the Genesis Restaurant, stabling for his horse, and forty dollars a month cash money which some members of the city council were still protesting, considering Frost an unnecessary expense.

Frost's daily ritual consisted of boiling himself a pot of coffee, checking the mail — if one of the twice-a-week stage-coaches had delivered any, looking into the Alhambra, then walking the dusty streets and oily back alleys which he did early and then late again in the day, avoiding the dry heat of midday. It wasn't a bad life, even if it was fairly pointless as the council had already considered.

Frost was still a young man, shading this side of thirty, but he had grown weary of the life of a drover. He had broken an arm and a leg on cattle drives, been shorted on his pay, worked sun-up to sundown moving stink-beef cattle from place to place under the blazing sun, sleeping on the desert floor where coyotes came into camp and tried to snatch away his boots while he slept. He had been kicked by steers, bitten by half-broken broncos and more than once been shot at by his own trail-mates. Both times the men had claimed they thought that they had seen Indians approaching the camp, but Frost remained unconvinced.

His present occupation lacked any excitement, which did not bother him at all. He had free cooked food every day, a bunk in the back of the jail where he could sleep off of the ground every night, and forty dollars pay a month, more than a cowhand got, for doing nothing but touring Climax twice a day, protecting it from some possible future bloodbath.

Plenty of men were worse off.

Life never really lets a man settle in, however; things can change in a moment. In Climax they started to change the day the first of the strangers arrived in town.

He was not a big man. He had his hat tugged low. His longish sideburns were silver, but tufts of red hair poked out from around the brim of his hat. He sat his weary-looking paint pony as if he were used to long stretches in the saddle. The holstered Colt revolver riding his hip looked as if it were comfortable riding there. The stranger looked up and down the street, appraising Climax expressionlessly. After a minute or two of surveying his surroundings, he walked the little paint pony toward the Alhambra Saloon — hardly a suspicious action for a man who seemed to have ridden long and would like something to drink

6

that would cut the dust in his throat.

Still there was something about the man that caused Giles Frost to frown as he watched him through the greasy front window of his office. Frost watched until the man had tied his horse to the hitch rail and gone into the saloon. Then he returned to his battered desk and stretched out his long legs, resting his boots on the desk top, tilting his hat forward a little to protect his eyes from the afternoon sun that was beginning to slant into the office through the window. Briefly he considered going over to the saloon to take a closer look at the stranger, but pushed the idea aside. 'You're just bored, Giles,' he told himself. Every stranger wasn't bringing trouble to Climax. He closed his eyes and dozed until sunset when he was due to make his evening rounds.

When Frost did awake there was none of that bit of a lag that many people have while orienting themselves to time, place and purpose. He had lived inside this pattern for so long that his legs were already swinging to the floor as his eyes opened. He could see the color in the sky — burnt orange and deep violet beyond the window pane; he was on schedule.

Going to the door, Frost went out into the still-warm early evening and began his methodical, patterned rounds. Rattling the locked front door of the saddle shop, he walked on. In front of the Alhambra Saloon he was a little surprised to see the paint pony the red-headed stranger had ridden into Climax still standing at the hitch rail, one hind leg cocked up. It was not an overly curious sight — many men had trouble walking out of a saloon once they had entered. Still the horse, which seemed to have been ridden far on this hot day, should have been seen to by now. Frost walked to the dozing paint, ran a hand along its neck and walked to the saloon door himself.

Peering in, he noticed the stranger at a corner table. He was seated with

8

Mayor Applewhite, whose bare dome gleamed in the light of the room and Charles Toledo, the saloon's owner. Now that was curious, Frost considered. Most often the greeting for a stranger to town was a nod — if any welcome was forthcoming — nothing more. Seldom was a wandering man invited to sit and drink with the mayor of Climax and its wealthiest citizen. Frost had only seen such hospitality offered one other time, when a railroad engineer appeared in Climax to discuss the notion of building a spur line to Climax, a project that went nowhere after the railroad man had examined the town and apparently found it sorely lacking.

Frost shrugged, there was nothing else he could do, and sauntered down the street. In the near-darkness, he caught his boot heel on the boardwalk's edge and nearly stumbled into Clara Finch.

'I saw you coming out of the Alhambra,' Clara gibed. 'You must have had a good time there.'

'You know that I just tripped,' Frost said with a sour smile. 'Why do you enjoy picking on me so much?'

'Because I don't like you, Giles Frost, and you know it.'

Frost did know it; what he never knew was why. Why did the small, dark-haired girl, who held a ready smile for everyone else, dislike him so much? Clara was a relief bartender at the Alhambra. Frost thought she was distantly related to Charlie Toledo, but was not sure. She did not dance, sing or wear revealing fancy clothes, but simply slapped down beer or whiskey on the bar — smiling at each and every man who placed an order.

Frost stepped aside a little, but it was unnecessary, Clara had already brushed past him on her way to another night's work. Walking forward, he moved toward the center of the street where there was no traffic and he was distanced from the sounds and smells of the Alhambra. And from Clara? He shook his head and glanced up at the silver half-moon riding high across the dark desert sky. Why couldn't the girl like him, at least a little, and why did Frost let her bother him so much? There were plenty of other women in town.

No, there weren't.

Not for him.

Gloomily he circled the Genesis Restaurant; there were now only two or three men in there, lingering over coffee. But the restaurant would not be ready to close. Its rush of business came after midnight when the hard-drinking crowd at the Alhambra finally decided that they ought to waste the last bit of silver in their pockets to try to save their stomachs for another day.

Frost entered the cross alley behind the restaurant and turned back toward the center of town, walking past the rear door of the feed and grain barn. A small dog, Luke Waylon's terrier, was barking inside the building, most likely at a rat in the grain bins.

The blank faces of the buildings were all familiar to Frost. The town was too familiar. He should leave, but he had no real idea where to go. Besides, as he grew older he found more comfort in familiarity than in change. In his time he had been beaten, shot at, snake-bit and crippled up trying to tame a bronco which had another idea about matters. Few of these things were likely to happen again — not in Climax.

The rear door to the Climax Stable stood open, probably for air on this warm, still night. Frost started that way, just to make sure that everything was as it should be. He called out before he entered.

'Waxy! It's Giles Frost! Everything all right in here?'

'It was until about a minute ago when some fool town marshal woke me up,' a grumpy Waxy Loomis said, emerging from the thick shadows of the stable's interior. Waxy's real name had been long-lost, perhaps by intent. Though the name 'Loomis' was painted on the front of the building, it had been left there by the stable's previous owner who had since run off into the wilderness with a Paiute woman, abandoning the place.

'Sorry,' Frost apologized. 'It's my job to check.'

'Always been your job; never have anything wrong around here,' Waxy grumbled. He was a beanpole of a man with a bulbous over-large nose decorating his narrow face. Waxy repositioned a suspender over his shoulder and walked nearer. 'What're you going to do about your horse?' the stableman asked.

Stunned, it took Frost a while to reply. He had not been paying much attention to his big buckskin horse lately, having little need to ride it. He had not exercised it enough, nor even taken the time to curry the animal, leaving those tasks to Waxy. Was the buckskin sick, dead?

'What do you mean?' he said finally. 'Is it all right?'

'Fat and sassy off free hay and grain

— that's what I mean, Frost. When are you going to start paying me for the horse's care?'

'Pay? Look here, Waxy, you know as well as I do that the horse is being maintained by the town of Climax for its appointed law officer.'

'That ain't what Mayor Applewhite told me last week,' Waxy said. The moonlight through the door showed his beady eyes and the glowering set of his face.

'What do you mean? That's always been the way things are done. The town pays for stabling and care of my pony.'

'*Did*,' Waxy agreed, 'but don't now. That's what Applewhite told me personally. If you two have a disagreement of some sort, talk to him. Me, I just need to get paid for the animals I tend.'

'There's some sort of mistake,' Frost said. 'I'll talk to Applewhite.'

'You do that,' Waxy said. 'Meantime, do you mind if I get back to sleep?'

Waxy turned his back and tramped back into the interior of the building,

14

muttering to himself.

Frost continued on his way. The evening had grown noticeably cooler. He tugged his shirt collar up. His nightly rounds would soon require a jacket. The moon had begun its downward arc; the stars were silver-bright against a background of black velvet, like display stones in a jeweler's display case. The blacksmith's shop was locked up tight, his shed secured. Mona Blake's little dress shop door was bolted. All as usual.

A slight breeze was blowing, just enough to ruffle the leaves of the half-dozen Cottonwood trees that stood at the west end of town. Frost decided to peek into the Alhambra Saloon once more and then return to his office. He took three strides along the alley before the world exploded, and pain like the impact of a sledge-hammer against flesh shocked his side and reverberated in his skull. He took two more steps, found he could walk no farther and slumped to the cold earth, the acrid smell of gunpowder hovering in the air.

Frost tried to claw his pistol from his holster although it could not have done him any possible good, but found that his fingers, his arm, refused to co-operate. He lay on his back in the alley, aware of the streaming of warm blood down his body.

He heard no further sounds. He tried to call for help, but no sound rose from his throat. He was looking skyward now, his chest rising and falling convulsively. He could feel dizziness and darkness trying to drag him down.

He raised an arm, grasping at the stars as if he might be able to use them to pull himself up. Then they blinked out and the night grew darker still and even more silent.

2

It was hot. Too damned hot. A fire was burning in his flesh. His brow was sweating, the stinging perspiration trickling into his eyes. He tried to raise his left arm to wipe it away, but found that it had been strapped to his body. The attempted movement only increased the heat and the accompanying pain. He had been shot — he remembered that now as he squinted through the blur of sweat toward the ceiling of a lantern-lit room.

'How bad is it?' he wondered aloud, expecting no answer.

'You'll make it,' a voice from some invisible soul replied.

'I'd forgotten how much a gunshot can hurt,' Frost murmured. Someone was there with him — wherever he was. As his thoughts began to clear he wanted to ask questions, needed to. He rolled his head on the pillow to look toward the corner of the small room where he believed the voice had come from. He almost choked on the word:

'Clara!'

'It's me, Frost.'

'What are you doing here? Or rather, what am I doing here?'

'Waxy heard a gunshot and found you in the alley. He ran to the Alhambra for help and I had them bring you over here.'

'To your place?' Frost asked, noticing now the predominant pink of the room, the bits of china on the dressing table.

Clara didn't answer. She was busy with a bit of cloth in a wooden hoop, embroidering some figures on white linen. Quite domestic. Frost was given the attention a restless dog might receive, no more. Except for what seemed to be a dampness in her dark eyes.

Frost tugged down the blankets covering him to ease the internal heat that was tormenting him and noticed that his torso was heavily bandaged, his left arm immobilized.

'Where did he get me?' Frost asked, trying unsuccessfully to lift himself from the bed.

'Who?' Clara asked with a meaningless smile, lifting her eyes from her stitching.

'Whoever it was that shot me,' Frost said stiffly, letting his head fall back onto the pillow.

'Who was it?' Clara persisted, returning to her needlework.

'I haven't an idea.'

Clara shook her head, clicked her tongue, placed her embroidery hoop aside. 'I haven't heard of anyone claiming responsibility,' she said, rising to her feet, smoothing the dark blue skirt she wore. 'But he just missed. The bullet went through your lower arm first and then into your side, just above the hip and below the lowest rib. No critical organs were hit.'

'I'm grateful for that,' Frost said, trying to grin, 'but whatever is missing down there, I used to enjoy having in one piece.'

'Well, you were — ' Clara broke off as both of them heard the loud rapping at her front door, out of sight from where Frost lay. 'If it's not one thing it's another,' she said. 'Stay here, I'll be right back.'

Frost supposed that was meant to be humor. He had tried again and found that he could not even sit up — not without an intolerable stab of pain. He had been right. Whatever was missing from his body, he had gotten used to having it in place. His arm was not too bad, although he could see blood still seeping through the bandages on his upper forearm. He breathed deeply and tried to readjust his position on the bed.

Clara was back with a white envelope in her hand. She waved it in front of his eyes. 'It's for you. Ken Baxter just brought it over.'

'Who's Ken Baxter?' Frost asked, his voice a little cranky. The pain was slowly returning. He found himself wishing he had never awakened from

20

his deep, dreamless sleep. Suddenly, somehow, he was cold now. He tugged the blankets up again.

'The courthouse clerk,' Clara said, seating herself again in the bedside chair. 'Don't you ever get over there, *Marshal?*' She handed him the letter. 'It's from Mayor Applewhite.'

'Probably condolences,' he muttered, struggling to open the envelope with one functioning hand.

'I don't think so,' Clara said doubtfully. 'Judging from the expression on Baxter's face.'

'Well, I don't know what else it could be, not just now,' Frost said as he removed the letter from the envelope and began reading it. His eyes narrowed, his face fell and Clara saw him stop his breath angrily and briefly grind his molars together. The hand holding the letter fell to the bed.

'They've fired me!' Giles Frost sputtered.

'They can't have. Not even you,' she added. Maybe that was meant to be humor as well, but Frost was not in a mood for it.

'It's true — take a look at this,' he said, handing her the letter, which Clara studied with the careful attention of a slow reader. She read a part of it aloud although Frost had just seen the note.

'Due to budgetary considerations, the council of the city of Climax has had to face certain painful decisions . . . it has been unanimously agreed that in these times of uncertainty, unnecessary expenses must be eliminated . . . ' Clara's eyes met Frost's with seeming sympathy as she read on.

'Of special interest to you is our agreement that the office of town marshal which is considered an extravagant expense in a town which is virtually free of crime, beyond the occasional petty infraction, should be eliminated.' She paused and began again, her eyes turned down. 'It is our belief that these few occasional misdemeanors can be satisfactorily addressed by the honest citizenry of Climax. A full-time officer is deemed unnecessary. Therefore we . . . '

Clara put the sheet of paper down on her lap. 'You're right,' she said. 'You've been shown the gate.'

'I know that.' It hadn't taken a second reading to convince Frost. 'So Waxy was right,' he said. 'He told me that the town was through paying for the care of my horse.'

'And?' Clara asked curiously.

'Waxy said that Mayor Applewhite told him that last week. Why should a stableman get the word before the man most affected by the decision?'

'Maybe to keep you from raising hell,' Clara said, rising again. She walked to the mirror and began fluffing her hair with a brush. 'Now you can't complain too loudly — not from the bed.'

'I wouldn't have complained anyway. It's their money, let them spend it where they like. The 'honest citizens of Climax' — whoever they might be

— can watch the town.' There was simmering anger beneath Frost's words. It wasn't the dismissal itself that rankled so much as the manner in which it had been carried out. It fit into the category of kicking a man while he was down.

And who had put him down? Who was the shooter in the alley?

'Well, I'm sorry,' Clara said, turning from the mirror to face him, brush still in her hand. 'I hate to see any man get a raw deal . . . ' Her voice faltered. 'I'm sorry as I can be, but you'll have to leave here before people begin to talk. And,' she added brightly, 'it's not like I even like you, Giles Frost.'

'Why do you keep saying that?' Frost wanted to know. His head was beginning to ache again.

'That I don't like you?' Clara asked, her lower lip pushing forward thoughtfully as she turned again toward her dressing table. 'Because it's true, Giles Frost. I don't like you and I never will.'

Oh . . . ' he said blankly. What sort of response could there be to that? He was still pondering the letter from the mayor. The timing of it was very odd. Firing him on the day after he had been shot. Was one occurrence related to the other in some way he did not understand? He asked Clara what she thought. Her mind was probably clearer than his was at this moment.

'Maybe they thought that after being shot it would make it easier for you to give up your job and move on,' Clara said. She gave a small shrug. 'I don't know, maybe someone figured if you were dead it wouldn't matter and no one would have to fire you at all.'

'You make it sound like a conspiracy,' Frost replied.

Clara shrugged again. 'It could be, couldn't it? Did you have any trouble with anyone in town last night?'

'Not a soul. I barely spoke to anyone.'

His thoughts returned to the letter of dismissal. 'Why? Why, Clara? Why would they decide to fire their town marshal?'

'They just told you,' Clara said, tapping the letter which lay on his chest. 'To save forty dollars a month plus whatever expenses you have.' She smiled crookedly. 'They can sell the jailhouse to someone who wants to turn it into a candy shop — anything. That would be money coming into the treasury, not going out for a service they've decided they don't need.'

'Even the smallest of towns, like Climax, needs some sort of law in it,' Giles Frost said, trying again to shift his position in the bed. 'Someone to wear the badge and prevent men from getting ideas of mischief just by his presence.'

'Yeah, you're pretty menacing,' Clara said, although she did have the grace to immediately look ashamed of her remark. 'Well,' she said, getting to her feet again, 'it's done now, anyway. There's nothing you can do about it.'

'I guess not,' Frost replied.

'There's no point in your staying around town now. I suppose you'll have to travel on.'

'I suppose so.'

She sat on the edge of the bed, her

liquid dark eyes meeting his, and asked, 'Where will you go, Frost? Have you even a place to go?'

He closed his eyes briefly and then nodded only slightly. 'I think so. I have to ask. I have a friend over — '

'You have a friend!' Clara asked with what might have been mock surprise. Maybe not.

Frost continued, 'A man named Anson Weaver has a small ranch east of here. I once did him a small favor. But it's been a long time ago and I haven't seen him since. He'll remember me, I'm sure, but maybe not with gratitude in his heart.'

'You can't ride right now,' Clara commented. 'What are you going to do in the meantime?'

'If I remember, in the agreement I signed, the town has to put me up in a hotel if I'm injured on the job. I've got a copy of the contract over at the jailhouse to refresh my memory . . . and Applewhite's.'

'I think you ought to stay clear of

those people,' Clara said. 'Mayor Applewhite and the other town council members.'

'So do I,' Frost agreed. 'That could only lead to harsh words being exchanged, but I have to stay somewhere — at least for a while.'

'Well, it certainly won't be here,' Clara told him definitely.

'No. I've already gotten that idea,' Frost said, his mouth turning down at her tone. 'I've got a few dollars stashed away. It hasn't cost me much to live the last few years. I'll find the contract, settle with Waxy for the keep of my horse, then . . . ' Then what? It didn't matter at that moment. Frost found he could no longer frame the rest of his sentence, found that he could barely keep his eyes open. He heard Clara cross the room, blow out the lantern and leave the room, but the small sounds were like those heard in a tangled dream.

* * *

The day was bright, the sun warm. Giles Frost swung his legs from the hotel-room bed, wincing a little as his body objected to even this small movement. The window to the room was open slightly at the bottom and the sheer white curtains fluttered in the dry breeze. After three days in the hotel, Frost was getting damned tired of his present way of living. He was tired of being only a part of the man he used to be, of hurting, of depending on others. He rubbed his head. It did no good to get angry. Standing, he reached for his boots. He now had the use of both hands at least. He and Clara — mostly Frost — had decided that it was doing no good to keep his injured arm strapped down. It had stopped bleeding days ago.

Clara had come by his room three or four times since he had taken up residence in the Royal, which was the presumptuous name of the single-story Main Street hotel. Someone, in a time now past, had invested his capital, time and hopes in the place which, like all of Climax, had failed to live up to its promise.

Frost's days now revolved around the hotel. He slept there, crossed the street for his free breakfast at the Genesis Restaurant, returned to the hotel to sit in the sun on the porch for a while before going back to his room to take an afternoon nap. The evening was much of a repeat. Skipping a midday meal which he did not need with the limited amount of exercise he was getting, he hobbled to the Genesis for supper, returned to the Royal, sat in the lobby, watching the few tenants of the hotel come and go, and walked to his room to go to sleep.

He waited for Clara each morning. She did not come. It was not that she was tired of nurse-maiding him. She just plain did not care about him enough to make him a part of her daily routine. If Frost ever forgot that, she was quick to remind him: 'I don't like you, Giles.'

One morning when she did arrive, looking pert and bouncy in a yellow dress, her dark hair gleaming in the new sunlight, Giles finally asked her.

'What have you got against me, Clara? Why don't you like me?'

She looked startled by the question. She straightened from what she had been doing — examining the bandages around his torso — and said, 'You've always been nothing but a bum, Giles. You had a job, a position if you will, but you just fell into that job. No one else wanted it. You haven't done a thing since you were appointed, and you never will, to better yourself. Now you don't even have that position. You will never amount to anything.

'I started working for my uncle in the Alhambra three years ago. I have been living under his roof for five years, since my mother died. I'm going nowhere; I have no way to advance. If I ever meet a man I admire, it will be because he has projects, ideas, ambitions. He will be moving forward, upward.'

'I don't see you going anywhere either,' Frost objected grumpily.

'That's because I don't want to make a move just to be moving,' she answered. 'Into what may prove to be a worse situation. When I go it will be to move upward, to better things. You,' she said disparagingly, 'do not even know what moving upward is.' She sighed in a disheartened way. She finished, 'And so I do not like you, Giles Frost.'

★ ★ ★

Frost also waited each day for the mayor or someone from the town council to come by for a visit. No one ever did. The desk clerk at the hotel had shown Frost a note which read: *Former Marshal Frost's bills are guaranteed by the city of Climax until the first of the month.* It was signed in a scrawl Frost recognized. *A.J. Applewhite, Mayor.*

He had been shown that note the day previous. It was now two days until the final day of his allowance. It was time to get moving — whether it was upward or not.

Once before this he had walked the length of the street to visit his buckskin horse at Waxy's stable. On this day after spending a while with the animal, he found Waxy in his broom-closet-sized office and asked about his bill there.

'You're good until the day after tomorrow,' Waxy muttered, not looking up as he swatted a horse fly on his desk. 'After that it's going to be cash on the barrel head.'

Heeding Waxy's words, Frost made his way to the faded white building which served as Climax's bank. The manager, Otis Johnstone, a usually cheerful, rotund man who habitually wore his spectacles low on his nose, met with Frost.

'I need to close out my account. I want to take all of my deposit in cash money — half paper currency, half hard money.'

Johnstone frowned; banks do not like people removing all of their money from their safes. Frost, as he had told Clara, had lived frugally as marshal, paying neither rent nor stable fees and taking his meals for free at the Genesis Restaurant. He did not drink heavily, nor use tobacco; as a result the forty dollars a month he had been paid over the three years he had served as the town's marshal had grown to a tidy little sum.

Johnstone returned after a few minutes with a small burlap sack. The money it contained was counted out in front of Frost.

'You're leaving town, I hear,' Johnstone commented as Frost placed the money back into the small sack and tucked it inside his shirt.

'That's right — they have no more use for me here.'

'Sorry,' Johnstone said with apparent sincerity, wagging his head. 'I thought you were doing the job well enough.' He smiled faintly. 'We never had a stick-up here while you were patrolling the streets.'

'Well,' Frost answered, 'I guess the town is moving forward. Me ... I'm just moving on.' Clara's words echoed in his mind.

'We'll be seeing you, Frost,' the banker said, as he walked to the door with him. 'Take care of yourself, will you?' Hesitantly he added, 'I don't know why, but I've got a nagging feeling that you're riding into more trouble. A lot more.'

What could the man have meant by that? Frost wondered, as he walked along the shady side of the street, returning to the hotel. Nothing, probably, just a notion that had popped into Johnstone's head. Still, the banker's words troubled him distantly.

Passing the Alhambra Saloon, hoping futilely that he might encounter Clara — although it was hours before her bartending shift — he noticed a trio of unfamiliar horses standing hitched in a row out front. It sparked his interest for a moment, but only for a moment. What did he care who came and went in Climax? What did he care about Climax?

In his hotel room he again counted his limited funds. There was $1,115 strewn out across the bed. Nobody's fortune, but a lot more than most men were walking around with in this time, this part of the country. Placing the money beneath the mattress, Frost lay back on the bed, convinced that he had not completely wasted his time in his stint as town marshal. The nickels and dimes he had saved here and there had added up.

He was tired from his short trip around town and his eyelids closed again. Morning would bring a new day — his last day in Climax. His last thoughts, a half-dream, were of Clara. In the dream she leaned over as if to kiss him, her eyes sparkling. Her lips were inches away from his, when she spoke.

'I don't like you, Giles Frost.'

'To hell with her,' Frost muttered, punching his pillow as he turned onto his side to stare at the blank wall beside his bed.

* * *

The big buckskin horse, long confined, moved under Giles Frost a little more eagerly than he would have liked. He was jolted in the saddle with each stride. He was relatively healthy despite the severity of his wounds. He was relatively wealthy and well mounted. He was also feeling suddenly aimless and useless. He walked the buckskin along the length of Main Street, Climax falling away from him. It was Clara he looked for along the street, but if she kept to her schedule, she would not be out yet. There was no reason to think she would make a special effort to see him on his way.

Frost did catch a glimpse of Mayor Applewhite, but the esteemed mayor ducked into an alleyway at Frost's approach. No matter — Frost had nothing to say to the man. He had nothing to say as parting words to Climax which he had tried to serve for the last three years. There was a certain bitterness riding with him as he reached the edge of town where the cottonwood grove stood and made his way out onto the rock-strewn desert beyond which lay the ranch of Anson Weaver, once a friend, a man who might give Frost shelter while he tried to patch his life back together.

To think that a single bullet had reduced him to the role of beggar and saddle tramp! No, he considered morosely, it had not been the bullet that had done the job, but the citizens of Climax. He had no anger toward them, but he would never forgive them their coldness in his time of trouble. He vowed never to return to that god-forsaken, crumbling desert town again. There would be no point to it.

To hell with Climax and all who dwelled there!

3

Anson Weaver's ranch was called the Liberty Bell. His cattle brand was a rough rendering of the famous bell. Where Weaver had come up with the idea, Frost did not know, and as he rode slowly toward the distant ranch, he realized that he knew very little about the man he was placing his hopes with.

Well, it did not matter. Weaver's ranch was at least a chance to find refuge while he healed and plotted out a true course of action. From what he could recall of the ranch, the Weaver house rested behind an outcropping of dusty granite on a dry grass wedge of land. To the east the grass grew more lushly and supported a fair-sized herd of beeves. Weaver was the solitary, close-mouthed sort who had always seemed to carry some secret sorrow with him which Frost did not feel familiar enough with the man to try to penetrate.

He knew that Frost had a son and young daughter — not so young now. Frost had met Weaver one summer day when the cattleman's horse had been snake-bit and gone down on a particularly parched bit of ground, pinning the rancher beneath it. Frost, then on his way to Climax because of the rumor that the town was in search of a law officer, had tugged the dead animal off of Weaver and taken him back to the home ranch.

Weaver had sworn undying gratitude, but Giles Frost knew how quickly such vows could dissipate. Gratitude did not often have a long life: a fact he had learned after loaning away much of his money to desperate men under flurries of flimsy thankfulness. Frost's father had once told him that if you loaned money to a man you might as well consider it a gift. The odds of seeing it again were slight. As were the odds of remaining friends with a man who had taken the loan as his due, who ducked around corners and grew resentful when you approached.

His father, he reflected, had not been a bitter man, but wiser than Frost had given him credit for when he was younger. He felt now that he could have used his deceased father's advice on several matters, though Frost had usually ignored any helpful words from the old man. It was funny how ageing could alter one's perceptions.

For the moment Frost considered only the long trail across the gray land. The sun rode higher and heated the day. Red-rock bluffs began to lift from the earth, forming long barren ridges. One of these resembled a cockscomb and went on for half a mile. Frost recognized the unusual formation and knew that he was on the right trail.

In the middle of the afternoon he crossed a rocky ridge and, as he looked below, letting his horse rest, he was sure he could make out the wedge-shaped valley where the Weaver house should lie. It was still terrifically hot and Frost felt the need for rest as much as his buckskin did. Under a trio of live oak trees not far from the cockscomb, he swung down from the saddle, loosened his twin cinches and sat against a slab of head-high red rock in the dry shade it cast. In other times it would have been more than unlikely, but with his arm still hurting and his side begging him for relief, Frost managed to fall asleep where he sat.

When he was awakened, it was by the steady clopping of a slowly ridden horse approaching him from the south. Stretching out his arm, Frost picked up his Winchester rifle from the ground and awaited the unknown visitor. The man directed his lean dun horse toward where Frost rested. He could see the man's long black mustache and narrow face — and the glint of sunlight on the badge he wore. The in-rider drew up some fifty feet away and called out with a simple:

'Ho! All right to step down?'

'Suit yourself,' Frost answered. He watched the man carefully as he swung from the saddle and came forward, rubbing his haunch.

'Not a lot of places to find water along here, is there?' Frost was asked.

'Not that I know of,' Giles Frost answered. 'Are you thirsty?' He nodded toward his nearby canteen.

'I wouldn't mind a swig, if you don't mind, but I was thinking more of my horse.' The stranger accepted the canteen from Frost and nodded his thanks. 'I suppose we can hold on until we get to Climax. Have you got any idea how far that is?'

'Something like twenty miles,' Frost answered. He was fascinated by the badge the man wore. Had he been summoned to replace him? Had the rest of what Giles had been told been only a bluff to ease Frost out of Climax? Did that make any sense?

The stranger took another drink of water and handed the canteen back to Frost, cuffing the droplets from his long black mustache. 'Thanks,' he said. 'My name's Tate, Barrett Tate, deputy sheriff out of Winona. I'm supposed to meet a man called Giles Frost in Climax. Do you know anything about him? He's the town marshal over there.'

What was this about, Frost wondered. He said, 'I think he's left Climax — for good.'

'Is that so?' Barrett Tate said, considering. He rested now on his haunches, his eyes narrowed from the glare of sunlight, studying Frost more closely.

Frost answered the unasked question. 'I'm Giles Frost,' he admitted. 'And yes, I'm through with that town for good.'

'I'm sorry to hear that,' Tate said. 'The sheriff thought you might be of some help to me, seeing that it was your town and you would know something about who might have come and gone recently.'

The deputy sheriff sighed and moved over to join Frost in the scant shade the rock behind him offered. After fanning himself with his black hat, gazing briefly into the distance, Tate told Frost, 'I'm

44

looking for a man named Charles Mansir. Ever hear of him?'

'No, I haven't. What's he look like?' Frost enquired, thinking of the red-haired stranger who had recently arrived in Climax.

'He's kind-of a bulky man, not tall but thick. He has dark hair and a brush mustache. He has a heavy brow, like someone had added an extra inch or so of flesh to it. It kinda droops down over his forehead.'

'I don't think I've ever seen a man like that in Climax.'

'You'd know him if you saw him,' Tate said. 'The sheriff wants him for murder among other things.'

'You're probably wasting your time riding to Climax,' Frost told him.

'You're probably right,' Tate sighed, readjusting his hat, 'but then, that's what most of my job consists of — long hours in the saddle followed by disappointment. It's not that hard for a man to get lost in this country if he has a mind to.'

'And stay lost?' Frost asked.

'And stay lost, but they usually resurface. They miss the good life, run out of money and come out of their holes to ride straight down the outlaw trail again. They're all creatures of habit. That's when I get them.'

'This Mansir is the dangerous sort, I take it. Not just a wild-eyed kid who got in trouble.'

'No. Not at all. Mansir has a finger in half-a-dozen criminal enterprises across the territory. I don't know why he flew off the handle this time and shot a man down in Winona. He usually stays well away from the action while his hired guns do the rough work.'

Tate rose to stretch and Giles Frost did the same, figuring he had better be on his way soon if he wanted to reach the Liberty Bell before dark. He told the deputy sheriff, 'The only stranger who's passed through Climax in weeks rode into town yesterday, if that's any help.' He went on to describe the red-headed man.

Tate's eyes narrowed, his lips compressed into a straight line as he listened.

'That might be a man I'm looking for as well. It sounds a lot like Dewey Skinner — he's a Mansir rider. I wonder why he'd be in Climax — did he look like he was on the run?'

'He wasn't trying to hide out,' Frost replied. 'I saw him cozying up with the two biggest men in town.'

'Then what . . . ?' Tate shook his head. 'I think I'd better find Dewey and have a talk with him. Something is going on in Climax which does not bode well for the town or peace in this county.' His look at Frost was now one of curiosity. Frost took the reins to his buckskin and swung aboard.

'I wish you luck, Tate,' Frost said. 'As for myself, I don't give a hoot about anything that happens in Climax from now on. I've retired from the business.'

Frost turned his horse's head eastward and rode away from the puzzled lawman who had his own pony started toward Climax. One riding to rescue the town from itself, the other escaping it. That was too dramatic, Frost considered. Tate had no idea what Dewey Skinner's presence in Climax meant — if anything. As for Giles, he was not fleeing the town in its time of need: they had told him that he was no longer welcome to even try to assist them in the event of any possible trouble.

Frost blocked the situation from his mind and started along the long rocky path toward Anson Weaver's ranch. In the distance where the grass was long and green, he could make out forty or fifty steers grazing around a water tank. They were no bigger than beetles at this distance, but seemed fat and satisfied.

Reaching the flat ground he saw a stone house set back against the base of the bluff and a log bunkhouse. A horse pen lay to one side of the log building, and a few of the horses lifted their heads with interest as Frost guided his buckskin in that direction. Early darkness was overtaking the land as the bluff cast a long deep shadow over house and yard. Most likely, this was the reason the house had been built there, keeping the full sunlight and heat of the desert day to a minimum.

He had arrived at suppertime, it seemed, for a bell was clanging from the side of the house and a few men started straggling toward the bunkhouse singly or in talkative groups. Frost started his buckskin toward the front of the stone house. A young man stepped out from behind the trunk of one of the cluster of closely growing live oak trees in the yard and signaled for Frost to hold up his horse.

The young man wore a yellow shirt and a shiny black leather vest. He had the beginnings of what might have been his first mustache above his challenging mouth. He wore a pearl-handled pistol on his right hip from which his hand did not stray.

'You might as well just ride out of here,' were the first words he said to Frost. 'We don't serve supper to saddle-tramps.'

'I wasn't looking to bum a meal,'

Frost said. There was a touch of amusement in his voice which seemed to irritate the young man. 'I rode in to visit Anson Weaver — he's an old friend of mine.'

'Must be pretty old,' the kid said, stepping forward a little, his hand still dangling in the vicinity of his fancy pistol. He eyed Frost carefully. 'I've never seen you before, I'm sure of that.'

'Well, it's been about three years since I met Anson. I was in the area and I thought I'd swing by to see him.'

'On business?'

'Not exactly,' Frost replied. He said no more. He didn't feel it necessary to answer the kid's probing questions. 'Mind if I pass?'

'What's your name?' the kid asked, his eyes still intent, his lips still sulky.

'Giles Frost,' he answered. In a touchy mood he demanded, 'What's yours?'

'Calvin Weaver,' came the surly response. 'Not that it's any of your business. Anson is my father.'

'Fine,' Frost said in a wooden voice. 'Now can I ride up to the house and talk to someone who has a scrap of courtesy?'

'I guess so,' Calvin Weaver said as if it pained him. 'Giles Frost — I seem to recollect hearing that name somewhere. Did someone send you out here?'

Frost ignored the question and kneed the buckskin horse forward. 'I believe you said I could pass,' he said. The kid, Calvin Weaver, had to leap back to avoid the buckskin's shoulder. Anger replaced the former sulky expression on Calvin Weaver's face. The kid was obviously not used to having his authority challenged.

Frost was thinking that he could have handled that better, but he hadn't been raised to think that it was necessary to soothe and pat every half-grown pup he ran across that wanted to snarl at him. There were two horses already tied to the hitch rail in front of the Weaver house. Frost swung down from the saddle and hitched his buckskin there as well. There was a watering trough located conveniently under the rail and the buckskin dropped its muzzle to drink. The sky had begun to purple to the west; the night birds began to stir among the oak trees.

Giles Frost stepped up onto the plank porch and walked to the front door, unsure what sort of reception he would receive. If Calvin Weaver's welcome was any indication of the way things were on the Liberty Bell, passing strangers were not particularly welcome here.

If Frost was not a stranger, he was the next thing to it. He might have saved Anson Weaver's life once, but that had been three years ago. The old man might not even recall his name. Frost had never seen Weaver or anyone he knew to be from the Liberty Bell in Climax. Of course, a lot of these old-time ranchers insisted on being totally self-sufficient in matters of food, clothing and entertainment.

And they were not happy about

sending ranch hands off to a place where hard liquor flowed. Men got into fights, bent to the will of local women, got thrown into jail or mobbed down, or simply stayed drunk for so long that they returned useless as cattle hands.

The door to the stone house opened; lantern-light fell across Frost's face.

A little blonde woman, as pretty as a music-box doll, stood facing him, lamplight shining on her hair causing it to look like spun gold. Was this whom Calvin Weaver was really trying to protect?

Her smile was tentative but warm, lifting the corners of her mouth charmingly. Her blue eyes stayed fixed on Frost's. There was a deep gleam in them — merriment, perhaps.

'Miss . . . ?'

'Ada is my name,' she said, stepping back to gesture him inside the large house. 'Everyone's welcome here.'

No one had told Calvin Weaver that, apparently. Accepting the hospitality of the more usual western greeting, Frost stepped into the house, removing his hat.

'I've come to see Anson Weaver,' he said, 'is he to home?'

'Yes, he is,' the girl, Ada, said. 'Was he expecting you, Mr . . . ?'

'Frost, Giles Frost. No, there's no way he could possibly know that I was coming.'

'You're just in time for supper,' Ada said, taking his hat which she hung on a pegged rack on the wall near the door. 'You can rinse your trail dust off at the pump out back, if you like. I'll tell Father you're here.'

'I wouldn't want to delay his meal,' Frost said.

'You won't!' Ada said with a short laugh. 'Father eats when he's hungry, stops when he's had enough. We're not very formal on the Liberty Bell.'

She led him down a narrow hallway to a side door. Opening that, she handed him a clean folded towel. 'It's right there,' she said, pointing to the familiar shape of an iron water pump.

She left the door open a little as Frost went to work trying to remove the worst of the trail grime from face, hands and arms.

The evening was still warm, the water ice cold. It was quiet across the yard, with only the occasional loud laugh from the bunkhouse where the cowhands ate their supper. Frost returned to the house, drying his hands along the way. A barn owl hooted at him from the roof of the house and then swooped away, searching for insects or small animal prey. Ada was just inside the house, waiting for him. She took the damp towel from his hands and watched as he rolled down the sleeves of his red shirt. She flinched a little as she caught sight of the bandage still wrapped around Frost's left forearm. Before she could say anything, Frost told her, 'I get a little careless now and then.'

Ada only nodded. It was none of her business and probably only of passing interest to her. She must have seen men with fresh wounds nearly daily on a working ranch. She beckoned him with a finger and said, 'Follow me.'

They retraced their steps up the hallway and then crossed the main room of the house with its plastered ceiling and heavy dark beams, Indian-made blankets thrown around as floor rugs, toward a door which was slightly ajar opposite, where flickering light from within indicated its use and the tantalizing scent of roast beef confirmed the room's purpose. When Ada opened the door, they could see Anson Weaver seated at the head of a long, candlelit table, busily sawing away at an inch-thick slab of roast beef. Weaver was gaunt, his cheeks sunken, his eyes looking less than bright. He had aged a lot since Frost had seen him last.

'Company?' the white-haired man said, glancing up.

'Yes, Father. I invited Mr Frost to supper.'

'Who? Do I know that name? No matter, have a seat up at this end of the table! Ada, you can sit across from him, if you will. That way I'll be able to hear the conversation.' The way Weaver said that made Frost think the old man must be having trouble with his hearing as well these days.

No surprise at his time of life; still, Frost did not enjoy the sight of a once-robust man inevitably surrendering to age. He walked with Ada to a place to Weaver's right and held her chair for her as she seated herself and gave Frost a sort of surprised and amused look as he performed this small gesture of civility. Taking the seat to Weaver's left he found the empty platter in front of him at once smothered in a huge wedge of roast beef and boiled potatoes. Apparently Weaver believed that a man who had come to supper should be quickly and plentifully fed.

Frost did his best to do justice to the meal. Weaver, having begun first, was finished first, and he leaned back in his chair, dabbing at his mouth with a linen napkin. His clouded eyes studied Frost without full recognition. Finally he asked, 'We know each other, do we?'

'Not well,' Frost answered. 'It's been a long time since we first met.'

'Frost, you say. You'll have to remind me, I'm afraid.'

'It was a long time back, Mr Weaver. Almost three years, as a matter of fact. Do you recall when your horse broke down under you and left you pinned to the ground up along Dos Picos Trail?'

'Do I not!' Weaver said strongly. 'I thought that was going to be the last day of my life. Did you ever try to crawl from under the weight of a downed horse? That was you who pulled me out, Frost?'

'That was me,' Frost said, cutting another bite of rare roast beef from the thick slab of meat he had been served.

'I remember that day well.' Weaver was looking now at his daughter. 'I'm pretty sure that I would not have made it if Frost hadn't happened along. I'd about given up. Hours of trying to free myself had left me in pretty bad shape.

The sun was high, my mouth was sandpaper, my strength was gone.' He looked at Frost again.

'I recognize you now, and I sure recollect the day. I told you then that if you ever needed anything just to call on me.' His cloudy eyes narrowed a little. 'Is that why you're here, Frost?'

'I'm afraid so,' Giles Frost admitted. 'I've come a beggar, needing a little help.'

'You'll get no help here,' the voice from the doorway said. Frost looked that way to see Calvin Weaver entering the room, still wearing his hat. 'I thought I made that clear to you outside: you're welcome to just one thing, Frost — an escort off the Liberty Bell.'

4

Ada looked at her brother in astonishment, Anson Weaver with severe disapproval.

The old man said, 'Calvin, do you want to come over here and feel my heart beating?' There was no response from his son. 'Well, then — it must be that I am still alive, and while I am alive, *I* say who comes and goes on the Liberty Bell.' The old man's voice softened a little, but not much. 'Frost here once saved my life. If you have no understanding of the feeling of gratitude, I do. He is my guest, and he is welcome here. Sit down and eat, or, if you dislike the company that much, go over and feed yourself with the bunkhouse gang.'

Calvin made a few grumbling sounds, but eventually seated himself beside his sister, tucking a napkin into his shirt collar. His eyes continued to bore into Frost's. Why, Giles could not have said.

He had made a few enemies in his time, but none who seemed to hate him so deeply and so suddenly.

'Your herd's looking fine,' Frost said, feeling the need to make casual supper-table conversation under Calvin Weaver's heated gaze.

'Well, we had a good rain this last spring — fairly unusual, as you know — and the grass came in fine. So we've been doing well enough.' Weaver asked, 'What about you, Frost? How have things been going for you? What have you been doing since we last met?'

'Staying over in Climax, actually. I was the town marshal there until recently.'

Ada's head jerked up and she gave Frost a startled little look. Calvin was shoveling food into his mouth, still glowering.

'What happened?' Calvin asked around a mouthful of potatoes. 'Did they get wise to you and run you off?'

'I left by mutual agreement,' Frost said, feeling a little defensive.

'That's what I said — you got fired.'

'I'm sure that's not what Mr Frost meant,' Ada said to her brother. Although it was the truth. Anson Weaver ended the brief exchange. Rising, he placed his napkin on the table and turned to Frost.

'It is my custom to take a little whiskey after supper, Mr Frost. Will you join me?'

Frost, who drank very little, was nevertheless happy for an excuse to escape the table. 'I'd be honored to share a drink with you, Mr Weaver.'

The two traipsed into a side room which was dominated by a long native-stone fireplace, a wagon-wheel chandelier and the mounted head of a massive grizzly bear. Frost stood before the mounted bear, hands behind his back.

'You don't see many of those around here,' he commented. 'Not these days, at least.'

Weaver handed Frost a glass of whiskey. 'The old boy wandered too far south. I would never have shot him except he had developed a fondness for Liberty Bell beef.'

'Did he go down easy?' Frost asked, sipping at his drink.

'Are you kidding!' Weaver shook his head. 'As I say, I hated to kill the big old rascal, but he was violating my rules . . . ' Weaver's thoughts seemed to drift away.

'What is it you need, exactly, Frost?' he asked, returning to the present.

'It's like this, sir,' Frost said, perching on the arm of a leather sofa, 'before they showed me the gate in Climax, I got shot up. All I need is a place I can recuperate for a while. I'm willing to do any work you need, but' — his smile went lopsided — 'I'm afraid there isn't much I can do right now.'

'Where'd they get you?' Weaver asked.

'My arm and my side.'

Weaver nodded. 'How long would you need, Frost?'

'Maybe two or three days, maybe a week. I'll be happy to work for you once I'm healed up. Or . . . ' he hesitated before saying, 'I can pay you something for room and board.' The thought of losing any hard cash was not pleasant to Frost. He had little enough and did not know where he could come by more at the present.

Weaver hoisted a hand and shook his head. 'Let's not talk of me taking your money, Frost. I don't need it, and I doubt you have much.' He blew out softly through his lips. 'Of course you can stay here. I don't forget a promise. And I made one to you.'

'Calvin might not like it,' Frost commented, taking another sip of whiskey.

'Oh, I *know* he won't like it,' Weaver said. 'But it's not his decision to make.'

'If I may say so,' Frost said, refusing a refill of his whiskey glass, 'the young man seems to have a good-sized burr under his saddle just now.'

'Yes,' Weaver admitted, sitting down on the leather sofa and crossing his thin legs, 'he does. I don't blame him entirely, but, well, we've had a little trouble around here lately and it's spoiled some of Calvin's plans for the time being.'

'I see,' Giles Frost said, although he didn't. 'What plans are those, if I may ask?'

'Well, let me begin this way: my lungs are no good any more, just plain shot is what they are. Tuberculosis is what they call it. I went to a doctor down in Bisbee, and he told me there's no cure. That I should live in a warm, dry climate — that was all that science knew to do for it. I laughed at him, of course. Where in the world is it warmer and drier than here? I guess I could move over to Death Valley, but I can't see how that would improve my health.'

'Probably not,' Frost agreed. 'But we were talking about — '

'That's when Calvin got this notion of his,' Weaver said, filling his glass again with amber liquid. 'He thought if he went to medical school he could learn how to cure me. He wants to study to be a doctor, you see.'

'That's an admirable ambition,' Frost commented, doubting that Calvin Weaver would have much of a bedside manner.

'Yes, it is. Whether or not he could learn enough to help me before I die is questionable at the best.' Weaver sighed, started to cough and squelched it. 'But he would at least have a profession he could be proud of.'

'You encouraged him?'

'Encouraged him and discouraged him at once,' Weaver responded. Frost's expression was of puzzlement.

'The nearest place Calvin could go to school is down in Saint Louis, Missouri. Miles distant, and expensive. He'd have to be gone for years, wouldn't he?' Giles Frost nodded agreement. 'Well, it came down to money then. I told Calvin that the only way I could finance him was to sell everything I own — and that is not something I am willing to do,' Weaver said with a faint smile.

'Or I told him that if he was sure he wanted to try it, I would give him his half of his inheritance now — I run four sections of land out here, Frost. I told him he could have his share of the ranch land now, try to sell it and use the money to go to medical school. Or — he would just have to hold on and wait to inherit. Of course when I go, half of the livestock and the property, including the house, will go to Ada. A woman needs a house more'n a man,' Weaver said.

'So what has he decided to do?' Frost asked.

'Near as I know, he hasn't. He'll get nothing from the cattle — and they are the main asset of any rancher. So I don't know what naked desert land is going for on the market now, but it's not as much as Calvin figures he'll need.

'Four or five weeks ago a couple of men from down south rode through and discussed a land sale with Calvin. They wanted the entire ranch, stock included, which isn't going to happen. I wouldn't hear of it; Ada wouldn't hear of it. So we've all been sort of arguing in silence. I love my son, but I'm not ready to live without my property. I won't let Ada agree to sell her real security. A few thousand dollars in cash money seems big now, but the years will chip it away quick enough. Unlike the cattle, which renew themselves every year.' Weaver slapped his empty glass down on a round mahogany table, shaking the crystal lamp which was placed there.

'That is my current situation, Frost. It's more than I meant to tell you, but I thought you were due an explanation as to why Calvin is acting the way he is.'

'I understand,' Frost said, although he didn't. Calvin's father had made his son a generous offer. Whatever he raised from the sale of two sections of land — 1280 acres — which admittedly was not prime real estate, would be enough to at least see him through a few years of medical school. In the meantime he could surely find some sort of work in St Louis to help with his bills, and if worse came to worst he would be welcomed back to the Liberty Bell even on a temporary basis while he saved enough toward further tuition to return to the Missouri medical school.

To Calvin it might seem like a long haul, and it was, but if he was that determined to become a doctor, it could be done. Calvin Weaver, like many young people (and probably an equal number of older ones), wanted everything and he wanted it now.

Life doesn't work like that.

Anson rose and paced the room. He looked tired now. Probably he had his two or three glasses of whiskey nightly after supper and then went off to bed. His expression when he turned to face Frost was apologetic.

'Sorry, Frost, I never even let you get around to explaining your problems.'

'It's not important,' Giles said, also rising. 'You've got the outline of it. The details are unimportant. Where do I sleep?' he asked, changing the subject.

'I'll have a room dusted and cleaned for you in the house tomorrow,' Weaver answered. 'For tonight — could you stand a night in the bunkhouse?'

'Of course. It wouldn't be my first time.'

'Fine. You'll want to see to your horse first, of course.' Weaver placed a narrow arm around Frost's shoulders. 'We've got a pretty good crew right now, but there are a couple of men I've taken on in the last week or so with round-up time approaching and few men available out here ... I don't know much about them, Frost, outside of the fact that they seem willing to work.' Walking toward the door, Frost turned and looked at Weaver's pale, sunken face.

'What's your meaning?' Giles Frost asked.

Weaver smiled weakly. 'I don't think you should mention that you used to be a lawman,' the old man said.

* * *

Frost found his own way to the front door. The others seemed to have gone up to bed. It was clear and warm outside, quite dark since moonrise was hours away. He untied his now-impatient buckskin and walked it across

70

the yard toward the red barn, which was set back well away from the bunkhouse to hold down the odor and flies there. He walked through the shadows of two facing oak trees which loitered in the darkness. There was no light within the barn and there seemed to be no one around.

Swinging open one of the high doors, he led the buckskin into the murky interior of the barn. He was searching along the near wall for a lantern when they hit him. Two assailants, maybe three — there was no telling in the darkness — swarmed over Frost in a tangle of arms, flying fists and boots. Bodies crashed against his and sent him heavily to the ground, driving the breath out of his lungs.

As the buckskin side-stepped away, Frost was gouged in the eye with an elbow, a knee was driven into his ribs. A fist rang off his skull over his ear and another caught his jaw with stunning force.

Everything in him told him to rise, to

fight back, but he hadn't the tools. His side had split open and was leaking blood. He could feel hot liquid seeping through his shirt. His left arm was nearly useless and he could not fend off the raining blows.

Instead of trying to fight the men, he curled up tightly into a defensive ball and simply submitted to another dozen blows which landed on his mouth, skull, ribs, back and belly. He could hear the men panting as they swung their heavy fists. He could smell the sour sweat of their bodies. Pain swept through him like a driving current and he nearly blacked out.

Just as he was on the verge of unconsciousness the men backed away to hover over him in the blackness. Frost could still not make out a face in the night. He did not know who had attacked him or why. He was aware only of confusion and pain. His attackers began to shuffle away toward the door. Before they went out of the barn, one of them paused to say across his shoulder, 'The best thing you can do, lawman, is hit the trail out of here.'

Then they were gone, their shadows merging with the darkness of the night. Panting, his head swimming, Frost managed to get to his knees where he waited, his hand pressed to the wound in his side. Slowly, painfully, he made his way to his feet and staggered toward the wall inside the doorway where he had expected earlier to find a lantern. His groping fingers located a hook on the wall where a lamp should have hung. His boot toe nudged something hard and light underfoot. He leaned over with great effort and his hand grazed the chimney of a lamp. Someone had moved it from its usual position to the floor.

Replacing the lantern on its hook, he fumbled a match from the box that sat beside the lamp and struck it to life with his thumbnail. The flame flared up, orange and blue and yellow, stunning Frost's eyes. He leaned against the wall as he adjusted the lantern. The horses in the barn had settled down after the fight.

His buckskin stood eyeing him with disgust and impatience.

Frost gathered up the reins to his horse and led it toward an empty stall, lantern held high in one hand. His head thudded and there was a ringing in his ears. It was a chore to unsaddle the buckskin with his torn side and injured arm, but he managed it, managed to find hay to fork into the stall, managed to hobble back to the barn door to replace the lamp.

He blew the lantern out and stepped outside, bruised and confused. One of his attackers had warned him off, calling him 'lawman'. Frost was not wearing a badge — how could anyone have known that? Was it some disgruntled trail hands he had angered in Climax at some time? He could recall no such recent incident.

The only ones who knew positively that Frost had been a lawman were the Weavers. Not Anson. Why would he bother to feed him and serve him drinks and then have him beaten?

Certainly not Ada. It had to be Calvin who had orchestrated this, but why? The young man didn't like him, but why defy his father when Frost had said he was leaving in a few days? That defiance could lead Anson to reconsider his generous offer to Calvin concerning the two sections of land that was his to sell if he so decided.

It didn't matter at the moment, Frost thought. Probably his confused mind was incapable of figuring it out just then anyway. He needed to sleep, to let his mind refresh itself. Even if he had decided to ride out, there was no way he was going to make it far on this night with his body in the shape it was in. Slinging his saddle-bags over his shoulder, he started toward the bunkhouse, which had quieted down by now as the cowhands let their meals settle and readied themselves for bed. Morning came early on a cattle ranch. He shambled heavily through the oak trees, panting as he walked.

The leaves crackled beneath his boot

heels. They rustled in the branches above him as a night breeze rose. The shadowy figure stepped from behind one of the trees and stood blocking Frost's way. He was not going to be taken again — Frost drew his Colt and thumbed back the hammer. The small noise was menacing in the night silence.

'Don't shoot,' said a familiar voice. The dark, indistinct silhouette threw its hands skyward. Frost took two strides forward, gun fisted tightly in his hand until the star-glow revealed the features of the stranger.

'Ada,' Frost sighed with relief. 'Don't you know you can get hurt wandering around in the darkness?'

'None of the men on Liberty Bell has such a hair trigger. What's happened to you?'

A little ashamed of himself, Frost holstered his .44 and walked to the blonde girl. He growled his response. He was still a little unsettled. 'Who says anything happened to me?'

'By the way you're walking, it's pretty

obvious,' Ada said. She lifted her hand and placed the back of it on his cheek. 'Now that you're closer, it's perfectly clear. You were in a fight, weren't you?'

Frost reflected and said dourly, 'Not exactly a fight — I didn't even make that out of it. It was a plain, simple beating I took. They jumped me in the barn.'

'Who was it?' She came nearer yet, her eyes reflecting starlight. There was concern in them.

'I don't know — I didn't see their faces, and even if I had, I probably wouldn't know who they were.'

'Well, I probably wouldn't either. We have a few new-hires on the ranch these days. Did anyone tell you that?'

'Your father mentioned them, but I can't see how anyone here could have known me well enough to have formed such a grudge.'

'Could it have been someone from Climax, then?'

Frost shook his head heavily. 'I can't see who.'

'But you say someone in Climax shot you,' Ada said. 'Maybe they followed you out here from the town. They couldn't do any shooting around here without drawing a lot of men, so they resorted to a silent beating.'

As conjecture went, that was solid enough, but the logic was strained. 'Maybe,' Frost only muttered weakly. He was staggering now without moving his feet, swaying from side to side.

'I'd better get over to the bunkhouse and find a cot,' he said.

'You will not!' Ada said forcefully. 'Not until we figure out what's going on around here. Come with me to the house,' she said, taking his hand with her own small soft fingers. 'Father told you that you can stay at the house. He just wanted to have one of the rooms aired out and dusted for you. Well, I think on this night you wouldn't mind a little dust when the option is bunking up with thirty men, at least some of whom may be holding a killing grudge against you.'

5

The silver moon illuminated the window as it rose over the long stretch of empty land which defined the extent of the Liberty Bell Ranch. Frost lay now on a wide soft bed near the window of the upstairs room. Ada had made a cursory cleaning of the little-used spare bedroom, attacking the cobwebs in the ceiling-corners with a broom until Frost stopped her, saying that he had not come to criticize anyone's housekeeping, but only to rest.

She had brought fresh sheets from a downstairs cupboard and remade the bed, Frost standing by uneasily, knowing that his side, injured again as it was, did not allow him to assist her. Finally when the sheets and blankets had been pulled back — a welcoming sight — Ada scooted up on the floor next to him and helped him tug off his boots.

Was she always this attentive? Surely not; she had recognized that Frost's injured side kept him from bending forward with any comfort, and decided to help. Nevertheless it was a welcome gesture.

With that done, Giles had risen to retrieve his saddlebags which he kicked beneath the bed.

Ada asked, 'What's in there?'

'All my worldly goods,' Frost replied, sitting down on the bed, thinking primarily of the $1,115 he had saved while working in Climax. At least he still had that. The men who had beaten him had been intent on that single purpose and had not searched his belongings or turned out his pockets.

He supposed he was still better off than he had been at other low points in his life. That was more than three years of a cowhand's pay. There might still be some hope for his future.

Ada's mind had apparently been fixed on more practical and immediate concerns. 'Do you have a clean shirt in your saddle-bags?' she wanted to know. 'You can't go another day in that one — it's pretty dirty from rolling around in the barn and it's torn at the sleeve and the shoulder.'

Frost glanced down with something like surprise at his ragged shirt. It was the last thing he had given any thought to. Ada, obviously, was a more practical sort. Frost had a vague recollection of rolling a black shirt and placing it into the saddle-bags. He told Ada that he thought so. Opening the saddle-bag he pulled the shirt from it. Ada took it and examined it with a touch of distaste. Apparently her idea of a clean shirt and his were different.

His eyelids were growing heavy. He supposed the dung-scented, blood-stained shirt he had on should be removed before climbing between clean sheets and so he clumsily peeled it off. Morosely he studied the trickle of blood on his side. The sheets would not be fresh and white come morning. There was nothing to be done about it just then. Ada had been studying the wound and the one on his left forearm with concern.

'In the morning we'll have to see to those,' she said, rising from the wooden chair. 'For now I guess you'd better . . . '

Frost did not hear the rest of the sentence, but he took Ada's intended advice. It was a bare moment after his head hit the soft pillow that he was sound asleep, even the pain winging away in dreams.

At first his night thoughts went nowhere. There was a herd of wild-eyed horses chasing him and an old man who inexplicably was trying to shoot him with a rattlesnake. As the night cooled and Frost lay curled up in his warm bed a different sort of moon-dream came over him. In it he was with Ada in full, golden sunlight beside an unknown pond where fish jumped from time to time. There were small red flowers in her hair, and she seemed to be laughing although there was no sound. Her head was thrown back; her mouth was open, showing even white teeth.

The ground beneath him seemed to tilt, and then a grizzly bear approached them on hind legs, wearing a dress and an apron. It walked directly up to Giles and lifted a pointing claw. Tapping him on the chest, the bear said in a familiar voice:

'I don't like you, Giles Frost.'

When he last saw the bear it had become Clara Finch and was running off through the forest, laughing and dancing as it went.

The light had changed as well. Now it was a brilliant sort of sun glare beaming through the dream forest.

Only it wasn't.

The sun had risen and it was shining brightly through the window of the upstairs bedroom where Giles Frost found himself awakening on the comfortable bed where he had spent his first night on the Liberty Bell Ranch. He tried to rise, but his movements were hesitant, tentative. He had been beaten pretty thoroughly. He lay back on the pillow to stare at the wooden ceiling, waiting for full consciousness to arrive.

Overnight the full coincidence of what had happened to him had somehow presented itself. That is — he had been shot at by an unknown gunman in the town where he had no enemies that he knew of.

Escaping to Liberty Bell, he had been attacked and beaten by a group of men who could have had no personal hostility toward him. Someone must have sent them, but who? His thoughts immediately focused on Calvin Weaver, whose dislike of Frost had been obvious. But Calvin knew that Frost was leaving shortly. Nor did Frost think that the ill-mannered Calvin would order such a beating in the face of his father's precise prohibition.

So the world had gone mad and across the world there lay a command that all who crossed the path of Giles

Frost were under an obligation to harm him. Frost smiled at his own fanciful thought. He yawned and searched around for his boots. He realized that it must be later than his usual rising time. The angle of the sun, which splashed rays into the room through the window, was higher than expected. It was past eight o'clock, that was certain. But then, he had needed the rest and he had no job to rise and attend to.

Oddly he found himself missing that — having an obligation, having a routine. Maybe Clara was right about him. Maybe he was lazy, willing to accept a little if his needs were provided for, not energetic enough to pursue a lot.

He halted himself in mid-thought. That was the third or fourth time he had had thoughts of Clara since leaving Climax — or five, if he counted her appearance as a bear in last night's dream which he suddenly recalled. Why? The little dark-haired girl was still present in his mind, even though she

85

had told him emphatically and frequently that she had no interest in him. No liking for him.

Even had he been willing to change, Giles Frost had no real conviction that he could ever change, become ambitious, bring home money in wheelbarrows. He was just not built that way.

As he rose with his boots on — getting into them had not been as much of a problem as he had feared — a mocking-bird scolded him from the windowsill and then fluttered away, apparently angry at someone having taken possession of something he had prior claim to. Frost smiled. He was still smiling when there was a tap at the door and, without waiting for his response, Ada Weaver swept into the room, looking fresh and pretty in a pale-blue dress, holding his black shirt on a hanger. Her blonde hair had been freshly arranged; she brought the scent of lavender soap and faintly of jasmine with her. She left the door open behind her and hung the black shirt over the back of the chair. It was newly ironed, Frost noticed. Recently enough so that it was still warm to the touch when he fingered it.

'Thank you,' Frost said. 'It seems I'm becoming a lot of trouble to you.'

'Not so much,' Ada said, sitting on the bed, hands between her knees. 'I didn't iron the shirt. Our housekeeper, Renee, did that for me. You'll see her around. She's a grand girl with a sad past. Her husband was killed on the westward trek. She was happy to take any job, and we were lucky to find her.'

Ada looked at Frost's bare chest, at the wound in his side which had quit seeping, at his scabbed forearm. 'We'd better clean you up a little before you put on the fresh shirt. Are you hurting?'

'Not as much as I had expected,' Frost said, and Ada gestured and then helped him stretch out on the bed, face up.

'Just lie still for a moment. I asked Renee to heat some water for me. She should be along momentarily.'

Frost lay back and waited while Ada

fussed with his wounds. Her fingers were gentle and light as they moved across his flesh. When Renee — a stocky, kind-looking woman with gray hair and a nervous smile — brought a pan of hot water, Ada carefully washed the wound in Frost's side, patting at it with a clean cloth until she had removed the scab and blood smear there.

'That doesn't look so bad now,' she said, sitting up, brushing back a strand of blonde hair from her forehead with the back of her hand.

'It was almost healed,' Frost said, 'before they jumped me.'

'You still don't have any idea who it was?'

'No more than I did then.'

Ada was now examining his forearm where the bullet which had passed through it had bored a hole but somehow missed bone and artery, slowing the slug's impact slightly before it ripped into muscle in his side. 'Your arm looks fine,' Ada announced, turning it over with her gentle hands, 'in a few days it should be good as new.'

'You think so?' Frost said. He had tried to work his fingers earlier, and it seemed to him that there must have been some tendon damage there. The arm felt heavily bruised as if it had been placed on an anvil and struck with a sledge. He hoped his arm was all right. It worried him more than his side. How would he ever — if it came to that — be able to return to working cattle, which seemed to be one of his few options?

'I'll get Renee back up here,' Ada said. 'I think it would be better if you wore a bandage around your side for at least a little longer. I'll need help to turn you over and wind it around you.'

'Maybe I can be of some help,' a voice from the doorway said. Calvin Weaver, his dark hair slicked back, a crooked smile on his face, strode into the room. His eyes flickered over the scene where Frost, bare-chested, lay on the bed while Ada fussed with his wounded side. 'You work fast, don't you?' Calvin said. There was a smirk on his lips, mockery in his voice.

'Don't talk to him like that,' Ada said, flaring up as she rose to her feet, a bloody cloth in one hand. She stood with her hands on her hips, challenging her brother.

'Who says I was talking to him?' Calvin answered.

Ada's voice rose to a shriek. 'Get out of here or I'll kill you!' she yelled at her brother. Before Frost could react, she had found his pistol and was holding it two-handed, aiming it at her brother. There was cat-like ferocity in her eyes. Calvin was leaning against the door sill, arms folded.

'I'm leaving,' he said. 'As for killing me, I suppose you will do it some time. Or at least try.' He spun away and exited. Ada lowered the pistol, trembling. Frost took it from her as she sat on the bed, holding her hands to her face, shaking her head.

'I'm so sorry,' Ada whimpered. She lowered her hands and caught Frost's eyes with her own blue ones. 'You don't know what's been going on around here

— between Calvin and me. His needling just caught me at the wrong time. I can't explain it all . . . '

'There's no need to,' Frost said, his voice mild, and he hoped soothing. 'It doesn't matter right now. For now,' he smiled, 'I just need to get out of this room for a while. If you could help me on with my shirt . . . ?'

Five minutes later, his hair roughly brushed, his gun slung around his hips, Frost, clad in his fresh black shirt, jeans and fawn-colored hat, walked down the stairs to the main room of the house. Looking past the dining room he could see that the door to Anson Weaver's office was open, and he crossed that way.

He found Anson Weaver at his desk. Weaver smiled briefly, and then rose from his chair. It was not easy for him, Frost could tell. The old man braced himself with the palms of both hands and levered himself upright awkwardly. Age was on its inexorable way to defeat him, but Anson Weaver was not going to surrender easily to it.

'Well,' Weaver said with forced heartiness, 'you're looking refreshed and spry this morning.'

Frost glanced at the brass-bound clock on the wall near the grizzly head, and noticed that as he had thought it was only just still morning. It was shortly after eleven o'clock.

'Sorry about coming down so late,' Frost apologized.

Anson Weaver waved a hand, palm outward. 'Oh, it's nothing, nothing. You've ridden far and you're just getting over your injuries.'

Apparently neither Ada nor anyone else had mentioned the beating Frost had taken the night before. Weaver sagged into his chair and smiled. 'Have you had any breakfast?' he asked. 'No, of course not. I'll call for Fat Boy.' At Frost's look of puzzlement, Weaver explained, 'He's Chinese. I don't have any understanding of that language. I thought he introduced himself by that name, but I could have been mistaken.

Anyway, it was easy to remember, and it was close enough to whatever his real name is, that he didn't mind.

'It's funny,' Weaver said, scratching his graying head, 'later I met a man who had traveled the seas and he told me that 'Fat' is not an uncommon name among the Chinese, and that 'Boy' is also common — so maybe, in my ignorance, I had it right all along.' Weaver continued, 'He's a small, bright-eyed man who's been my cook for years now. I don't suppose you've seen him around.'

'No, I've only met Renee.'

'She's a pleasure to have around,' Weaver began. 'When I first met her — '

He was interrupted by the sound of a door opening and closing, of leather boot heels approaching across the wooden floor of the dining room and the appearance of a trail-dusty cowboy, his hat in his hands.

'What is it, Martin?' To Frost he said, 'This is Martin Campbell — my ranch foreman.' Frost turned and the two shook hands perfunctorily. Campbell was a well set-up man of thirty or so, with dark serious eyes and black flyaway hair. Just now he looked worried.

'Why aren't you out captaining the herd?' Weaver asked.

'My damned horse threw a shoe. I had to come back and let Banger replace it,' Campbell said as if it were of no importance. 'Thing is, sir, on the way back in I saw a group of drifters making camp down along Sabine Creek. I've no idea who they are, or what you wanted me to do about it — at the moment with my horse about to go lame, I could do nothing, of course.'

'We'd better go out and have a look at them,' Anson Weaver said, rising more fluidly from his desk, reaching for a rifle on a nearby wall rack. They were already moving toward the door when Campbell told his boss, 'I met Calvin along the trail and told him about it. I think he was going to go over there alone.'

'That's a bad idea,' Weaver said. 'But Calvin is an impetuous man.' Anson glanced back across his shoulder at Frost. 'Are you well enough to come along, Frost? We could use an extra gun.'

Frost only nodded and followed in their wake. As they crossed the dining room, Martin Campbell was still talking. 'There's four or five of them, sir. They are probably just drifters heading for Climax to get their fill of whiskey.'

'Or men who have had their fill of whiskey and are now looking for trouble,' Anson pointed out as he opened the front door. 'Either way, they're going to have to move along.' Weaver's face looked drawn with concern now, but there was determination in his cloudy eyes. Frost followed the two along toward the barn.

They could hear the sound of a hammer beating against iron. 'Banger' it seemed was the Liberty Bell's farrier. They entered the barn and saw a big, balding man in a leather apron and shirtsleeves, holding up the left rear leg of a sleek-looking, little steel dust pony, nails in his mouth, hammer in his hand.

'About finished, Banger?' Martin Campbell called out.

The farrier looked up sourly. 'No, I ain't about finished,' Banger said, after removing the horseshoe nails from his mouth. 'I had to pull off the right rear shoe as well — he was about to lose that one too. Don't you ever check your horse over, Martin? I've got to rasp that hoof and fit a new shoe, and . . .'

'Mind if I take the palomino, then?' Campbell asked, brushing past him.

'It belongs to the ranch, don't it? 'Course I don't mind.'

Campbell immediately began saddling a three-year-old palomino pony while Anson Weaver went back along the row of stalls to lead out a sturdy-looking bay horse. Frost went looking for his big buckskin, and found it standing in the third stall back, hay frosting its muzzle, its eyes wary. He saddled it with effort, moving carefully so that he wouldn't tear his side open again. By the time he was finished the other two men were already in the saddle and waiting.

They trailed out into the bright day, passing through the oaks in the front yard and heading their horses east, toward the grazing grounds. The grass was heavy, and as they proceeded Frost began to see scattered, sleek cattle, their heads bowed to the graze. They all wore the Liberty Bell brand — a bell-shaped figure with a crack sketched across it. There were no men nearby. Far away to the west, beyond the gathered herd Frost could see the forms of half-a-dozen men on horseback. Too far away to talk to or call out to. The three investigators rode on in silence until they came to a broad, shallow river which he took to be the Sabine Creek. Nothing like the broad Sabine River down in Texas after which the creek must have been named, but free-flowing and hearty in its passage. Splashing across it on horseback, Weaver told Frost, 'The creek's the only difference between the south pasture here and the north which I have offered to give to Calvin. Grass is sparse up there and dependent on the rainfall. I wasn't going to offer him the south range. If I did, then I'd have nothing.'

The horses scrambled up the muddy bank to reach flat ground again and Frost answered, 'If he can find a buyer, that much acreage will still profit him enough to let him go to school, no matter how dry it is.'

'That's my hope,' Anson Weaver said. He was slightly bent over in the saddle, his face looking strained. Martin Campbell was well ahead of them now, bent forward across his palomino's withers as if with urgency. Frost hurried his horse a little bit, and Anson Weaver followed suit.

There were low hills now on their right; widely scattered pines and a few white oak trees grew there. Campbell was talking to Weaver when Frost again drew even with them.

'We'll talk to them, all right,' Campbell was saying. His words were now bent by a rising wind. Campbell's voice was angry. Weaver just nodded his head as his foreman spoke. 'I doubt they'll want to go to shooting when we've got thirty hands on the range behind us, but you never know.' He suggested, 'How about if Frost there circles the knoll and watches for anyone trying to get away from us?'

Weaver looked to Frost who nodded his understanding. Campbell said, 'We're just going to talk to them, Frost, but if they start shooting, throw your sights on any man who tries to escape from the camp.'

'All right,' Frost muttered. Then he turned the horse's face northward again and rode toward the tree-stippled knoll, the dry wind in his face. Up toward and then among the trees, Frost guided the buckskin using only one hand on the reins. His Winchester repeater filled his other. He rode warily, not knowing this country. The wind whistled through the higher branches of the pines and shuffled the leaves of the oaks. Looking back, he could no longer see Anson Weaver and Martin Campbell.

Oddly this probing ride into an unknown region caused him, briefly, to miss Climax where every street or alley, each building was familiar to him. Perhaps that had been his element. No matter — he was here now and never returning to that town.

He crested the knoll and looked down upon a bend in the river across the sage-studded land. He waited there, letting his horse breathe, trying to survey any possible escape route the intruding men might make use of. He decided he should make his way toward the creek so that if a battle did erupt he would have a nearer shot.

He clicked his tongue, nudged the buckskin forward with his knees and started down from the knoll.

Fifty feet on he was blown out of the saddle by a rifle bullet.

6

Frost was on the ground again. He had been tilted away from the rifleman as the dark figure on horseback charged down on him from the trees, and the bullet had glanced off his left shoulder and burned the back of his neck at the base of the skull. That was the hit that had put him into a spin and caused him to briefly black out. And it was the wound that hurt. Searing pain rushed gleefully along his neck and set off fireworks in his skull. His vision was a blur when he opened his eyes to try to fight back should the ambusher try another shot.

His horse had danced away in fright, and now Frost lay against the warm, rocky earth, his fingers and legs twitching but doing nothing to allow him to rise, no strength to draw his revolver. Horses charged downslope from out of the trees once again and Frost was ready to give it up. There was no way he was going to fight off a trio of armed men — or a pussy cat — in his state. He opened his mouth to cry out but only a muffled croak emerged from his lips.

A single man with a rifle now hovered over Frost. He did not speak a word. It seemed he was about to when two more horses arrived.

'Who is it?' he heard a voice ask.

'It's Frost,' the man standing over him said. This, Frost was sure, was Calvin Weaver. How had the man been so near to the shooting?

'Frost?' one of the men who now circled around him on horseback cried out. Frost could not see who it was through the veil across his eyes, but as the man dismounted and came nearer, Frost was able to recognize the voice and faintly the face of Anson Weaver. Crouching down beside him, Anson muttered, 'Son, you do have a way of getting yourself in trouble's path.'

'I hurt pretty bad,' was what Frost thought he said, but the words in his mouth became a jumble of disconnected sound.

'Get him back to the ranch,' Anson Weaver said, rising.

'What about the trespassers?' Someone — perhaps Martin Campbell — asked.

'We'll catch them another day — if they're stupid enough to stay around,' Weaver said. 'We'll bring a dozen hands with us next time if they come back. For now, get Frost back to the house. Calvin, lend a hand!'

Frost was lifted onto the back of the buckskin horse. Someone lashed his feet to the stirrups and he was led off, reeling in the saddle, supported by unseen hands as he rode down the knoll and out onto the grasslands.

Who had shot him . . . ?

It seemed there was an army of invisible men out there waiting to kill him at every turn. Calvin Weaver had been the first man to him, so he must have been quite near indeed. If it were Calvin, why? He knew the kid didn't like him, but that much? He considered that it might have been one of the suspicious band of men they had found camped on Liberty Bell land, but if that were so . . . Frost shook his head; thinking was too difficult just then. With his head bobbing back and forth on his neck he allowed himself to be led across the long grass flats toward the distant house.

He wanted to . . . Then he blacked out again.

He wanted nothing when he awoke in the same bed he had slept in the night before. Nothing but to remain asleep and take the basic comfort of its cool sheets. He had been rolled onto his side. So that his wounds could be treated, he supposed. He wanted to reach up and touch his shoulder and neck to feel for bandages, but the project seemed so difficult that he gave up the idea and simply closed his eyes again. There were no dreams in his sleep, only a rolling, roaring sound as if he were trapped in a barrel in a tornado.

When he awoke again the sound had subsided; his vision was clearer, but pain arced through his body. Was he never going to get the chance to heal up? His head was clotted with stunning pain. His shoulder might have been on fire. His side had flared up again after the fall from his horse and even his arm throbbed in complaint.

That was it! He was not going out riding, traveling, stirring, unless someone set the house on fire. He had had it.

'I am one miserable piece of dog meat,' he mumbled, and astonishingly someone answered.

'You've done your best in difficult situations for a long time now.'

He pried his eyes open and saw a patiently smiling Ada Weaver sitting in the wooden chair in the corner, her nimble fingers busy with a piece of needlework.

'What time is it?' Frost asked, without attempting to raise his head from the pillow — he doubted that he could.

'Does it matter?' the blonde girl asked.

'No, I suppose it doesn't,' he answered, closing his eyes again. He did not fall off to sleep then, but keeping his eyes shut seemed to make being awake easier somehow.

The next time Frost managed to pry his eyes open it was evening and Ada had returned with a bowl of hot bean soup. He managed to prop up his body enough to feed himself. He took that as victory, aware of how that feeling of achievement defined how much of an invalid he really was.

He was just plain sick of it: of the bandages, the bed, the special treatment. What he wanted was to rise now, dress and ride out onto the open land. Of course, that would require him feeling as he normally did — a long time ago. His body could not be expected to serve him as he wished it to. Not now.

His older wounds had been getting the time to heal themselves, but the new ones were far behind in the process. His shoulder felt horribly bruised, and he could feel it leaking blood if he moved too quickly. As for his head: the back of his neck ached constantly and he had thunderous headaches.

Ada tried to encourage him by saying once, 'Another couple of inches and your head would have been blown clean off.'

'That would have ended it all, at least,' Frost answered. 'I'm damned tired of the ache, lying here uselessly . . . the sheer pain.' Still he did not know, so he asked Ada one bright morning. 'Who was it who shot me, Ada?'

'One of the trespassers making a break for it when Dad, Martin and Calvin dug them out.'

'I didn't see any of those men . . . why is it that Calvin was the first man there? Within seconds, actually.'

'You can't think that my brother shot you!'

'How can I not think it?' Frost responded. 'He doesn't like me. He wants me out of his hair — why? I'm not sure.'

'I'm sure you must be wrong,' Ada said. She was straightening up the room, drawing back the pale flimsy curtains to allow the morning sunlight to filter into the room.

Frost only nodded. He was not so sure. 'I've got to get up and out of this room, Ada. Somehow.'

'I can get Renee or Fat Boy to help me get you down to the front porch. You can sit in the sun.'

'As idle as ever, like an old man or a convalescent.'

'Which is what you are,' Ada reminded him. 'You decide what you want to do.'

Anything, he decided, but stay there flat on his back. Ada, perhaps guessing his mood, returned later with the small Chinese cook, Fat Boy. The man's dark eyes were concerned and seemed to hold sympathy.

'We take you down,' he said confidently. Frost wasn't so sure that it could be done: his head still exploded with violent, blinding pain now and then, and blackouts threatened. His legs, however, were sound and so he nodded and tried to sit up. It was a dizzying journey down the staircase with Fat Boy under one arm, Ada under the other. As he stepped out of the house, the brilliant sunlight stunned his eyes and he felt himself go wobbly as they guided him toward a wicker chair resting on the porch. The porch canopy shaded his eyes while the rest of him was left in warm new sunlight.

'If you want anything, yell,' Ada said. She was puffing a little from the exertion of bringing him down. Fat Boy offered to get him a cup of coffee, which he accepted. He did have one request.

'I'd like to talk to your father, if he's around.'

'He may be up; maybe not,' Ada said in a tight voice. 'He's been weakening. Coughing up a lot of blood. The tuberculosis . . .'

Frost only nodded his understanding. He had seen the consumption hit other men, watched them fade away as they wheezed and coughed their life out. Despite the good intentions of Calvin — if that's what they were — he would never be able to minister to his father in time to stop the old man's decay. Frost wondered idly if that was what made the young man so angry. There is no anger like the anger of frustration that arises when there is simply nothing to be done.

Fat Boy brought Frost a cup of dark, hot coffee and served it with consoling sounds as the morning crept onward. The shadow cast by the awning crept lower, which suited Frost as the day grew warmer and then desert-hot.

Was he, like Anson Weaver, now condemned to sitting in a porch chair, reflecting on his life?

What life? Frost thought, momentarily angry. In his younger days he had behaved badly, roistered and brawled, believing that those wild episodes

110

would be something to look back on in the years to come. He could see now that he had just been a fool. He had never owned land, a house, never been married, or had a son or daughter. He had never done a thing to be proud of.

Except being marshal of Climax. No matter what Clara Finch had thought of his job, it had given him quiet pleasure to walk among the citizens of the town knowing they trusted their security to him. True, there was not much of a threat to anyone living in that out-of-the-way desert hamlet, but Frost had felt useful there and at least vaguely welcome and embraced as a town fixture.

To hell with Climax! he thought with a sudden surge of anger. In the end they had just turned him out like a dog. And look where that had led him. A drifter, a battered and bruised bit of desert riff-raff.

Fat Boy had come again to refill his coffee cup. The man's bright eyes smiled.

'You be back soon,' the Chinese said. 'You one tough man.'

Frost smiled his thanks for the complimentary opinion, wishing he believed Fat Boy's words. A severe headache struck again just then, a blinding flash of pain, and he wondered if he were doomed to suffer the debilitating flashes for the rest of his life. Maybe he had been right when he told Ada that it would have been better if his head had been blown clean off back along the Sabine, if he had to endure these blinding headaches for the rest of his life . . .

Three mounted cowboys raced past across the yard, weaving their way through the oaks there. They whooped and shouted and laughed. Their high spirits were evident, and Frost envied them their youth and exuberance.

Studying the ranch yard now, Frost saw another group of hands — four of them — standing at the shady side of the barn. These four were older, their faces sullen. They stood together deep in conversation. There was no indication that they were preparing for work on this afternoon. After a while they broke up and wandered away separately. A lawman's suspicions rose in Frost's mind habitually, but almost as quickly, he disabused himself of the notion of speculating. It was none of his concern. And he was no longer a lawman, but only a —

What was he?

The thought again invaded his mind. What was he? A broken-down saddle-tramp with even the roof over his head provided by a man for whom he had once done a small favor.

Fat Boy again emerged from the house. He told Frost, 'The boss, Mr Weaver, he say he would like to see you in his office now if you can make it so far.'

Could he? It seemed daunting, but he thought he could make it that far with Fat Boy's assistance. He had been wanting to talk to Anson Weaver anyway, and if the old man was now up and alert, it seemed a good time to do so.

By the time Fat Boy had leveraged Frost into a chair in Anson Weaver's office, Anson had already seated himself as comfortably as he could and waited with his cloudy eyes containing what Frost took to be an expression of warmth toward him.

'How's the recuperation going?' Anson asked.

'Well,' Frost answered, 'I feel this morning that I am going to live.'

'That's something, I suppose,' said Weaver, whose expression indicated that he himself did not have that much optimism. As if to emphasize that, Weaver removed a handkerchief from his breast pocket and commenced coughing, long and spasmodically, his shoulders trembling, his eyes watering as he brought up blood from his ravaged lungs. When he was finally over the fit, Weaver folded the handkerchief carefully and placed it away.

'I am sorry, Frost,' the old man said.

'Can't be helped — when you have to cough, you have to cough.'

Weaver shook his head. 'That's not what I meant. I apologize for asking you to go along with us out to the Sabine. You were in no shape for that kind of ride, and all I did was get you shot up again, very nearly killed.'

'I felt I could help, otherwise I wouldn't have gone along.'

'Yes, you would, if you had clung to the idea that you owed me something.'

Frost made an indefinite gesture with his hand. He knew that Weaver was intent on apologizing, but it really hadn't been his fault at all. 'That's all in the past now,' Frost said. 'There must be something else on your mind.'

'There was,' Weaver said, with a small after-shock of coughing which he restrained with a fist placed in front of his lips, 'until I saw how you are this afternoon.' He leaned back and sighed. 'Men are continuing to drift onto the Liberty Bell from all over.'

'Saddle-tramps looking for jobs at round-up time,' Frost suggested.

'Yes, that was my first thought. I've

told Calvin and Ada not to turn any prospect away, since we will need a full crew. Ada took on five men from Texas yesterday. Calvin has been away, you see.'

'Where is he?'

'I've no idea,' Weaver said, shaking his head heavily. 'So Ada, following my orders, hired them on.'

'I've seen a few who I take to be new-hires hanging around.'

'Martin Campbell hasn't had the time yet to sort them all out, show them the lay of the land and assign them.'

'Something about the situation is bothering you?' Frost commented.

'Well, yes, Giles,' Weaver answered. His expression became serious, almost glum. 'As you know, new men are welcome at this time of year. Cattle can't be rounded up and driven to market without them. But, on the other hand, too many new men can be a concern. Are they here to work for the brand, or because they have their eyes on the herd itself?'

'I guess that could happen.'

'It has more than once,' Anson Weaver said. 'That was where my futile idea was spawned.' Frost eyed the old man with enquiry. Weaver explained, 'I had the idea that you could be put up in the bunkhouse with these men and look around, listen, try to get an idea of how honest they were. But . . .'

'But that idea went out the window when I got shot again.'

'Yes. Banged up as you are now, no one is going to believe that you are a part of the crew. You can't fall in with anybody out on the range, get them to loosen up.'

'No,' Frost agreed. 'That's beyond considering. There's one more matter, Anson — at least one man on this ranch knows that I was the town marshal in Climax. Remember? One of them called me 'lawman' when I took that beating in the barn.'

'I know,' Weaver said heavily. 'My idea was all a pipe dream. I haven't been thinking too clearly lately.'

'All you can do is put a cap on the hiring and alert Campbell and the other old hands you trust to keep their eyes and ears open.'

'I know it. You're right,' Weaver admitted heavily. 'Was there something else you were thinking of, Frost?'

'Well, yes,' Giles Frost answered. 'I'm of no help to you staying around here. In fact I'm making more work for everybody else. Keeping Renee and Fat Boy from their regular duties, taking up Ada's time . . . I want to be moving on, Anson. How long a ride is it to Bisbee?'

'Bisbee?' Weaver said, juggling surprise and inevitability in his mind. 'Do you think you can make it that far, Frost?'

'I don't know. Maybe if I take it easy. I feel like this: I have a better chance of surviving out on the desert than I do on your ranch just now. Someone wants to kill me, Weaver — you know that as well as I do.'

Weaver thought deeply but not for long, then he nodded. 'It's a day's ride to the Cochise County line, then another day into Bisbee . . . two days' ride for a healthy man on a good horse.' He eyed Frost doubtfully, but Giles gave him a small grin and answered.

'Well, I've a good horse.'

7

The dawn light was bright, igniting small sparks in the dew spread across the grasslands, the wind in his face cool and unwelcome. Giles Frost guided his buckskin horse through the hills, moving away from Sabine Creek and the Liberty Bell Ranch. The big horse moved easily, almost eagerly beneath him. Giles was just hoping to hold on. He didn't belong in the saddle and he knew it. Rising that morning in the near-darkness he had stumbled and fallen back onto the bed, setting off the now-familiar bright whirling rowels of a blinding headache. It took him ten minutes while he sat there holding his face in his hands before the pounding, roaring headache subsided enough for him to try it again.

Dressing was a muted agony, saddling his horse a trial for Sisyphus. At last mounted, his headache slightly subdued, he crossed the yard of the house, passing through the oak trees to reach open land. He didn't see anyone at all waving goodbye.

Why Bisbee? He considered as he rode. Well, why not Bisbee? Perhaps by the time he reached the town he would be in better shape, able to find some small job he could handle, although that seemed unlikely at the moment when simply remaining upright in the saddle was a severe task. Perhaps he thought, he could find a well-qualified doctor in the larger town. He had no idea. All he knew was that he had nothing to contribute on the Liberty Bell; he had only been taking from them.

And there was a very good chance that remaining there would have led to his death. Twice he had been shot at with that intent; they could not miss forever. Again he tried to piece together the puzzle of *why* someone would want him eliminated. It seemed to have something to do with the fact that he had been the law in Climax, but that made little sense since he was now obviously and permanently free of that job. That, in turn, did not match the piece of the puzzle as to why he had been relieved of his job in the first place. Mayor Applewhite and the rest of the town council had given him no hint that they were thinking of letting him go. Among other citizens, the banker Otis Johnstone had told Frost that he had appreciated his way of going about his job. Frost had never received any negative comments about his policing of the town.

Except for those from Clara Finch, of course — but since the woman liked nothing about him, these did not count.

By the time Frost had zigzagged his way up the first rank of hills to where the land flattened and the grass grew sparse and yellow, the sun was at mid-morning height and growing warm on his back. The brighter sun had brought the return of his headache.

Fortunately this time it was no debilitating shock but only a slowly throbbing reminder that he was not going to be able to shake free of it as easily as he had ridden from Liberty Bell into the wild country.

The buckskin horse plodded steadily onward across the hard, dry earth of the upland valley, Frost clung to the pommel, reeling in the saddle. He did not try to guess the time by glancing up into the hot crystal of the sky, but determined that he had to stop. It was time for that no matter what any clock might have said. He began peering into the brightness of the day, searching for a shady place to clamber down and rest.

Ahead of him, a mile or so away, he saw a low landform, too crumbled and formless to be described as a mesa, which it must once have been. Time, extreme weather and erosion had gnawed away at its original shape. It stood low and flat against the skyline, a red, rapidly ageing desert form. Frost headed his horse that way. Somewhere along its folded, broken flanks there had to be some place that was sheltered from the constant heated sunlight. Frost needed to get out of the heat and, nearly as much, to escape the shimmering light which was toying with him — ready to explode into brilliant, overwhelming pain behind his eyes.

Not for the first time Frost considered that he had been foolish to even attempt this trek, but he remained equally convinced that to remain where he had been was to court death. The broken mesa was farther away than it had seemed to Frost, for, by the time he had reached its foot, the sun was already lowering behind its rim rock, spreading deep, dry shadow out onto the desert. Not particular in the least, Frost began searching for any split in the mesa's wall, any narrow notch where he could step down and bathe himself in shadow while he rested.

When he found it, it was unexpected, although he had walked his horse, surveying the mesa's flank carefully. The canyon was very narrow, the entrance difficult to detect from a few yards away. The cleft extended upwards to the very rim of the mesa; the narrow trail to its interior was almost dark in this light. It wound for a short way as Frost could see and then seemed to widen as it bored its way into the broken hill's depths. Hopefully, Frost turned his horse that way.

Watching out for loose stones or crumbling ledges overhead, Frost rode into the notch, following a turn to the right and then a sharper elbow to the left, the walls of the passageway so near at one point that they rubbed his legs as he eased through. Not fifty yards on, the trail opened up, and beyond him, Frost saw a long, slender valley where a lone oak tree stood spreading its wings over the dry earth.

It was there that Frost saw a riderless horse standing over the sprawled, motionless figure of a man.

Frost halted the buckskin, drew his

Winchester from its sheath and carefully looked around the narrow valley. Then, squinting against the sun which pierced the notch, he crossed the dry grass toward the still figure of a man. The standing horse — a young palomino with a nearly all-white face — lifted its head to watch them as they drew nearer. The buckskin's hoofs caused the brown grass to crackle. A warm breeze funneled into the canyon, swaying the branches of the live-oak tree.

Frost remained in the saddle for a long minute, feeling a new headache beginning to build at the base of his skull as he looked down at the motionless man.

'Are you going to swing down, or are you just enjoying the sights?' the man on the ground asked. He rolled over and Frost saw the Colt revolver in his hand.

'You looked . . . I thought you were probably dead,' Frost said. 'I didn't know who else might be around.'

'There's just me so far as I know,' the stranger replied, sitting up and rubbing his head, which was sprinkled with dry grass and burrs. 'I couldn't go on any more without rest.' The man stood and dusted his jeans with one hand. The other continued to grip his Colt. 'I didn't even bother to try to make a pillow or unsaddle my horse. I just had to close my eyes for a while.'

'Been riding long, then?' Frost said.

'Long enough. From Winona in a day and a half. I can't seem to find the road to Climax.'

'There isn't one,' Frost said, 'not of the sort that most people would call a road.'

'Is that so?' The stranger was meditative. His clear brown eyes studied Frost with speculation. 'I take it then that you know the area.'

'Well enough,' Frost answered. He was growing dizzier and the pain in his head was building again. 'Excuse me,' he said, and he dismounted in an awkward slide. 'Had to do that before I fell off my horse,' he apologized, seating himself cross-legged in the oak tree's moving shadows, looking up at the stranger whose eyes now showed concern. The man holstered his revolver and squatted down beside Frost.

'What is it, brother? Have you been shot?'

'Not for a few days now, actually,' Frost muttered, trying to smile. 'I'm on a lucky roll.'

'Do you need some water?'

'I'd appreciate it. There's two full canteens on my horse.'

The stranger strode to the buckskin, retrieved a canteen and returned, crouching down beside Frost to hand it to him. 'Sorry if I seemed a little over-cautious,' the man said, when Frost had finished his drinking and replaced the cork in the canteen, 'it's been a long ride and I'm in unfamiliar territory.'

He sat down beside Frost, who had closed his eyes against the shifting golden sunlight and the blinding headache he knew was coming.

'My name's Orlando Marsh — most folks call me Lando. I'm a deputy sheriff out of Winona. I'm looking for one of our men who was sent up here last week and hasn't returned.'

'Barrett Tate,' Frost said. The stranger, Lando, stared in return.

'How did you know that?' Lando asked, with a hint of suspicion in his tone. Frost looked up and smiled.

'I met him along the trail. He couldn't locate Climax either.'

'Barrett Tate?' Lando asked in surprise.

'That's the name he gave me. Thin-faced man wearing a long black mustache.'

'That's Tate, all right,' the stranger said, sitting on his heels. 'That must have been over a week ago. What do you do? Just wander aimlessly around the land?'

'Pretty much,' was all Frost could think of saying. He couldn't explain everything that happened to him on the Liberty Bell. It was too long a story.

'What did Tate tell you?' Lando asked, wiping his hand across his crop of brown hair. There was still grass and stickers in it. He replaced his hat, tilted it back and waited for Frost's answer. The deputy was wary as he should be, not knowing what was happening around him in this part of the country.

Neither did Frost, come to think of it He told the deputy, 'Tate said that he was looking for a man named Charles Mansir who had committed murder down in Winona. He said that he had been sent up to contact the local town marshal to try to set up a plan to find and capture Mansir.'

'That's right — a man named Frost. I wonder if Tate ever got through to Climax to meet up with him?' Lando said.

'I know he met up with him; I don't know if Tate got through to Climax.'

Lando frowned. 'I don't get your meaning.'

'I'm Giles Frost. But I haven't been marshal in Climax for quite a time.

130

They fired me before I ever met Tate, which was not that far from where we are now. He rode on, and I suppose he made it to town unless someone who knew he was coming was waiting along the trail.'

'I don't see how anyone could have known he was coming.'

'Neither do I. That's all I know, Lando. I haven't seen the man since. I haven't been back to Climax since.' Blessedly, the throbbing in his skull had begun to subside as the sun fell lower and its direct light no longer reached the canyon floor.

'You'll ride with me to Climax, won't you?' Lando said, rising to his feet.

'Why would I wish to do that?' Frost asked. 'Besides, I'm on my way to Bisbee.'

Lando studied the man before him and asked, 'What makes you think you'll even make it there, Frost? You don't seem to be in the best of shape.'

'Look, Lando,' Frost said with some heat, 'I don't know if I can make it there. I'm just trying to take my best shot at remaining alive. Returning to Climax doesn't do a thing to improve my chances of that.'

'You're afraid to go back?' Lando asked, studying Frost with speculation.

'No, but unlike you, I haven't got a reason in the world to try.'

'Do you want me to give you a few?' Lando asked a little harshly. 'Here's one, Frost: I've been watching you, and you haven't got a chance of reaching Bisbee in your condition.'

Frost began to get angry, started to argue, but he couldn't. Lando was probably right. He had been thinking along the same lines himself.

'What else?' he asked peevishly.

'A fellow law officer came here needing your help. You refused him and now he's missing.'

'I wasn't a fellow officer by then. There was no help I could possibly have offered. Is there something else you can say to convince me?'

'I don't know if I can convince you of

anything,' Lando drawled. 'But you should be considering the position you have left the town in. You must at least have a few friends there, people you care about.'

'Do I? I didn't see anybody raising a big ruckus when I got the boot.'

'They didn't know yet what was going to happen to them. They probably still don't,' Lando responded.

'Man, you are miles ahead of me,' Frost said, 'or am I too slow to keep up with you? What are you talking about?'

'We think they want Climax,' Lando said.

'*They* want Climax! Who wants it? And why would anybody in this world want that pitiful sun-beaten collection of desert shacks and shanties?'

Lando sighed, crouched down again and as his fingers fiddled with a few blades of dry grass, said, 'Charles Mansir, for one. There was some talk in Winona that Mansir wanted to turn it into an outlaw stronghold. The man who did the talking was a member of the gang Mansir gunned down in anger, winning him that murder warrant.

'It wasn't like Mansir to do the dirty work himself, so we started sniffing around a little. We confirmed the gossip. That rumor had been heard by more than one man. Then one day Dewey Skinner rode out, heading in this direction, and Barrett Tate said to me, 'That's it. They're going to make their try.''

'I met this Dewey Skinner, a red-headed man?' Lando nodded, and Frost went on. 'What's he got to do with anything?'

'He was the advance man for Mansir, the way we figure it. Sent up by his boss to look things over, see if the ground was fertile for a takeover, find out what kind of law they had in that town, make friends with a few of the local big-shots if possible, grease a few palms . . . '

Frost frowned. The last time he had seen Dewey Skinner he had been sitting in the Alhambra Saloon talking to Mayor Applewhite and Charles Toledo.

Frost had wondered at the time what the desert rat could have in common with Applewhite and the town's most prosperous citizen, Toledo.

'They probably decided that you couldn't be bought,' Lando was saying, 'and arranged to have you dismissed.'

'And shoot me!' Frost said angrily.

Lando shrugged. 'That could have been Dewey Skinner's work. I'd guess it was. That's the way he conducts business. He wouldn't have wanted to just wait patiently for you to go away.'

'It's all incredible,' Frost said numbly.

'Life's incredible,' Lando said, rising again. 'The point is that Charles Mansir will be sitting in the catbird's seat soon if he isn't already. Climax will be his town, an outlaw town, and I doubt any lawman will ever be able to get near him after that happens. Not with all of his men gathered there. That's why Deputy Tate wanted to get there as quickly as possible . . . that's why I do.'

Lando stretched his arms, glanced at the darkening western sky and asked,

'Are you going with me, Frost? Once Mansir gets the town in his clutches, the honest citizens won't have a chance. Those who can will probably flee. But there will be innocents left behind, women and children living in constant fear beside Mansir's army of outlaws.'

People like Clara Finch?

By the smoky crimson light of sundown the two men rode steadily on toward Climax. Lando had judiciously removed the badge from his shirt. Frost did not wear one either, of course, although Lando had sworn him in as a deputy sheriff. It did not matter if they were wearing stars or not, there would certainly be no welcome for them in Climax where Charles Mansir's outlaw empire was taking root.

Pausing once on high ground along the way, Lando turned in his saddle and pointed out a party of five horsemen illuminated by the last flicker of the dying daylight on their backtrail.

'New enlistees,' Lando commented. 'They'll start coming now — old comrades, men on the run, gun hands needing work and a place to lie low. You never realize how many outlaws there are out here until they gather together.'

'It could be that they're just drifters headed for the Liberty Bell to find round-up work,' Frost commented.

'The *what?*' Lando asked with genuine surprise.

'The Liberty Bell Ranch,' Frost explained. 'It's just a few miles east of here. That's where I was riding from. They've been taking on a lot of new men with round-up approaching.'

'I hope they have an idea who those men are,' Lando said grimly. 'You know, Frost, they could be a bunch of thieves and robbers who have decided to bide their time until Mansir notifies them that the deal for Climax is done.'

Frost felt his chest tighten a little. If that were so, who would there be to prevent the outlaws from ransacking the house and taking what money Anson Weaver might have hidden in it? Calvin? He was gone, apparently. No one knew where. That left Ada and the foreman Martin Campbell along with a few long-time ranch hands.

Coward that he was, Frost thought, he had ridden off and left them to their fate out of fear for his own life. The same as he had done with Climax after being gunned down. What was there to do now but choose his place of dying?

'We'll have our look now,' Lando said, gesturing toward Climax where lanterns were being lit across town. 'I hope to God they haven't killed Tate, but it seems likely, doesn't it? Ride with your Colt loose in your holster, Frost: I'm thinking you're going to need it, and soon.'

8

The town looked familiar: dry, dark and dingy as ever when the two men approached it in the waning glow of twilight. The uproar of Climax could be heard long before they reached the town limits. Shouting, banging, glass breaking. Along Main Street the town was rollicking. Climax, which had formerly been deep with grave-like shadows at this time of the evening, was now very much alive. Its revival, however, had not been natural and healthy. Some dark magic had revived it.

The Alhambra Saloon, of course, was brilliantly lighted. It was the focus of the activity. Men fought and yelled obscenities. In front of the saloon a knot of men, marginalized by the space limitations within, raised beer mugs and whiskey glasses, whistled and whooped at nothing Frost could see. Four mounted men riding abreast raced up the street wildly, their ponies lathered. Frost and Lando were forced to jerk their horses aside as they met them.

A man on the roof of the Alhambra fired his pistol into the air and then hurled a whiskey bottle at the knot of men in front of the saloon. From an alley near Waxy's stable more shots could be heard. Men firing at targets or randomly discharging their firearms. The horses stabled there could be heard complaining. Frost heard enough cursing to last an army regiment a month as they rode past. Hardly a man looked their way. They were just two more shadows in the night.

Frost and Lando had reached the end of the street when they paused to talk opposite the Genesis Restaurant. Inside, a pair of rambunctious men had begun to tussle, knocking over a table. Irene, one of the waitresses Frost knew, could be seen holding her hands to her head in dismay.

Halted in the shadows of the oak grove across the street, Lando asked,

'Does it look like you left it?' There was no answer from Frost. Lando added, 'It seems you weren't doing that bad a job for the town after all.'

'I don't know what I could have done about all of this,' Frost said, leaning on his saddle horn as he appraised the wild street of Climax.

'It wouldn't have happened all at once. With a few good deputies you could have kept them moving on.'

'Maybe,' Frost said quietly. 'What have you got in mind, Lando? What are we to do now?'

'The first thing I need to do is try to find Barrett Tate, if he's alive. To do that I think I'll have to go to the saloon where men are bound to be talking and see what I can pick up.'

'I'm known there,' Frost said. 'The bartender, or maybe the regulars, or the owner, Charles Toledo, might call out my name. That would be the end of that.'

'Yes, it would,' Lando agreed. 'I didn't mean for the two of us to go together. You're in no shape to do so, anyway. I'm going by myself. No one knows me, at least I hope not, and with the influx of so many men, a stranger won't be noticed. One among many. Do you have someplace you can go? I mean, it's your town, you must have a friend.'

Frost shook his head heavily. All he could think of was riding back to the Liberty Bell, but he didn't think he could stay in the saddle for that long and he doubted his trembling buckskin horse could make it that far. His next thought was of Waxy's hayloft, but he remembered all of the shooting down at that end of town. Besides, it was likely that a bunch of newly arrived outlaws had already commandeered the loft as their sleeping quarters.

'I've got nowhere . . . ' Frost said. And it was a desperate admission. He had nowhere to go in all of this world and no friend to cheer him on his aimless journey. He studied the ravages of the town he once took his bit of pride in protecting. Up the street four or five wild shots were released into the night sky.

'You'd better find a place,' Lando said with concern and a little impatience woven into his tone of voice. He was obviously anxious to start off looking for his friend, Deputy Tate. 'If you don't you're just going to sit that saddle until you tilt out of it and end up sleeping wherever you happen to land.'

'I know it,' Frost muttered. He could feel one of those blinding headaches beginning to build at the back of his skull. 'There might be one place . . . ' If it could be done. If she had enough pity in her heart to forget for one night that she did not like Giles Frost. Lifting one listless hand to Lando, he started the buckskin forward toward the narrow path where Clara Finch's little cottage stood.

At the moment that he had started that way a rider was approaching the town from the east. Frost glanced that way and caught a glimpse of the man straddling a recognizable sorrel horse. Frost blinked, wiped his eyes and stared back through the tree-shadows as he watched the man ride past toward the center of town.

He knew him. Calvin Weaver. And what would the kid be doing in Climax with his father dying and the ranch in a confused state as it tried to organize a round-up? Frost watched the man on the sorrel lose himself among the shadows and the uproar of the street and simply shook his head. Only days ago Giles Frost had known and understood almost every man he met, had known every inch of his assigned domain, down to the names of the hounds. Now, it seemed, he knew nothing at all of what was happening around him — the little he did comprehend had been told him by Lando. Once comfortable in his ignorance and place in the world he was now an ignorant wanderer in a world of chaos.

Frost had no liking for this new world, and no solution for it. How could his world have ended so quickly? The world still stood, of course, but it was inhabited by savages. He was still alive, but he rode his buckskin on like the displaced spirit of a man. Ahead of him now was the faint glow of a lantern through a single window of a small cottage along the trail. The only place left of the old world for him to try to find some comfort. A place where he was unwanted and unliked. Like some forgotten ghost he approached the cottage of Clara Finch.

He had thought about her as he rode, worried about her. He knew she did not work the late-night shift at her Uncle Charlie Toledo's Alhambra Saloon because the crowd of late drinkers could grow unruly and even menacing for a young woman. But now — when the line between the late drinking, rowdy men and the more controlled early drinkers seemed to be erased with the arrival of gangs of heedless wild men from off the desert, what would she be able to do for a living?

He drew his horse up before Clara's cottage, still reeling in the saddle. He had been wounded so much lately . . . he only wanted a place to lie down, a small return of his old energy. What he did not want was to join a probably futile battle to try to retake Climax from the outlaws. Leave that to men like Tate and Lando. With a small jog of his conscience he recalled that he had allowed himself to be sworn in as a deputy sheriff. Would this never end? His stupidity, apparently, was boundless.

He swung down from the stirrups and made it to the ground as gracefully as possible. It wasn't all that graceful and he was glad there was no one around to see his awkward landing. He was aware enough to remove his saddle-bags containing his life's fortune from the buckskin before he headed toward the doorway.

Frost limped, stumbled, continued on through the dusty darkness toward the porch of Clara Finch's tiny house.

The door swung open before he had mounted the steps. Clara herself appeared in the doorway, back-lit by the lantern within.

'Holy cats!' she said in an exasperated voice. 'Could my bad luck get any worse?'

He swayed and stepped up onto the porch, saddle-bags slung across his shoulder. He tripped on the second step and nearly stumbled into her.

'Sorry,' Frost said. 'I was wondering . . .'

'Quit wondering it,' Clara snapped, 'and get inside the house before you fall down and I have to drag you in. What in the world have you done to yourself now?'

Frost staggered forward. Crossing the threshold he placed an arm over Clara's shoulders to keep from falling. Her face was expressionless as she guided him into the small living room. Frost halted mid-way across the room and looked up at the white-plastered ceiling which fascinated him for the moment and then flared with red and violet lights. Something struck him on the back of his neck and a giant hand shut the door on consciousness.

'Well, now what have you done?' the voice out of the mist asked.

'Me?' Frost asked. There were so many people running around inside his skull that he wasn't sure who she was addressing. Gradually the ghosts settled into a puddle of dream-memories and the mist cleared away. He was alone on the bed. Clara was watching him from the wooden chair in the corner.

'Haven't we done this before?' Frost asked, still uncertain of his footing in reality.

'Yes, the last time you did something stupid,' Clara answered. 'What did you do this time?'

'I was trying to help . . . '

'And you were a big help, weren't you?' Clara hissed out the words, sighed and rose. She turned her back to him and walked to the window to open it. A faintly moving breeze crossed the room.

It was still early in the morning then, for the breeze was cool.

'Have you seen what's happened to your town?' Clara demanded, standing over him with her hands on her hips. She wore a ruffled white blouse and a pale-green skirt this morning; her dark hair had been pinned up neatly.

'I saw,' Frost said, closing his eyes again. Even the moderate brightness of the sunlight through the window was painful as some nerve behind his eyes was touched by it. 'But I can't see what makes it my town. I was fired, remember?'

'Some people retain a sense of loyalty,' Clara said archly.

'I guess I'm not one of them,' Frost muttered.

'Look, Giles,' she said, coming nearer and bending over him. 'The town is being held hostage. Who knows if they might decided to burn it down tomorrow?'

'They won't. They need it for a hide-out.'

Her eyes widened. 'You do know something about all of this, then!'

'A little. Probably not much more than you.'

'My Uncle Toledo is nearly ruined. He's selling twice the whiskey and has three times the mess to clean up every day. I used to think the old collection of whiskey-bums was bad, but these men . . . I have no job now,' she told him. 'Uncle Toledo put me out the back door and told me not to come back.'

'Wise of him.'

'Yes, but what am I to do now?' Clara asked.

'Leave,' Frost suggested, opening his eyes again so that they met the clear blue eyes of Clara. Frustration was evident on her face.

'That is something you'd suggest,' she shot back. 'That's what you tried — and look at you.'

'No use in scolding me for doing what everyone wanted me to do,' Frost said mildly.

Clara went on as if he hadn't answered her, 'I haven't any money and nowhere to go. Would you like me turned out onto the desert like some Biblical nomad?' She paused. 'Uncle Toledo isn't the only one who's being ruined by these intruders. Waxy's stable is losing money every day. These new men don't pay for stabling their horses. They don't pay for their feed. His stable is a flop-house at night for them all. They continue to drink and to smoke in the hayloft, he told me. One night they'll burn the place down. Luke Waylon's Feed & Grain business is faltering — these outlaws just take what they want. The same goes for every shop on Main Street. The bank has closed. There's no one putting money in, and no one Otis Johnstone would trust enough to loan a dime to. He's taken the bank's money out and hidden it somewhere. They tried to rob him three separate times on the first day they swarmed in.'

'And I'm to blame for all of this,' Frost grumbled.

'Oh, maybe not. But you sure haven't been any help,' Clara complained.

'I wasn't here!' Frost replied bitterly. 'Or don't you remember? I was not necessary. I'm sorry if I don't share your sense of loyalty to those who undermined me. You are more noble than I.' His sarcasm was lost on Clara, whose thoughts had raced ahead.

'Someone could ride and get the army, or . . . oh, what can we do, Giles? We need some sort of help. A few county sheriff's deputies if nothing else. Maybe if someone could make it through to Winona and talk to the sheriff.' Her eyes looked hopeful and frantic at the same time.

'They're already here,' Frost told her. 'The sheriff's deputies, I mean.'

'I haven't seen any! How could you know that. Giles?'

He smiled weakly and told her, 'Because, I'm one of them.'

Clara stepped away from the bed, her face one of pale astonishment. She shook her head slowly back and forth. 'What are you talking about? Are you just trying to cheer me up a little, or making some sort of stupid male brag? You haven't had the time to even ride to Winona and back, much less to get yourself hired on as a deputy sheriff.'

'Believe what you want,' Frost said. 'You always do. Leave me alone and let me get a little more rest, will you? I think I'm getting better, but trying to talk to you isn't helping my head any.'

'All right,' Clara answered with equal sarcasm. 'I'll go out and watch for the posse to arrive. Shall I tell them that you're in here?'

'Tell them that my soul has passed away,' Frost muttered.

'I think it probably has,' Clara said, 'some time ago. It's no wonder that I do not like you, Giles Frost.'

The door to the room slammed shut and Frost was alone. The slight breeze continued to sift into the room, though it already seemed a little warmer. Frost rolled onto his right side and tried to sleep some more in this safe haven where he was an unwanted guest. With all of his concerns it was no wonder that a daylight nap was impossible. After half an hour or so he gave up on the idea and swung his legs to the floor to begin dressing.

Mentally he checked his battered body over. Bullet-shot left shoulder: aching and a little stiff. Not too bad. His side: pretty much healed now, scabbed over. Forearm: very stiff but not sore. He checked the fingers on his left hand and found that they still functioned. No permanent tendon damage, then. Torso: still aching if he moved too quickly in the wrong way, from the beating he had taken in the barn on the Liberty Bell.

He decided that he was in surprisingly good shape all in all, except for . . . the moment he thought about his head wound his skull began to throb with dull, numbing pain. He sighed. At least it was intermittent now, and he was not blinded by the hot flashes of light. At least, not so far this morning. It gave him some hope that the damage was ebbing.

Dressing was still a painful, clumsy experience, but he managed to get upright and ready reasonably well. Walking out into the dark interior of the small house, he flicked his gunbelt around his hips and buckled it on. Should he say good-bye to Clara or simply slip away?

The decision was snatched from him. Clara was sitting in the stuffed leather chair in the living room and opposite her, on the matching leather sofa, sat Lando and a blood-soaked, bruised and battered Barrett Tate.

9

'Ready to ride?' Lando asked with an amused smile. Tate's eyes were swollen and blackened. Whatever he had been through it had not been a welcome greeting to Climax.

'Hello, Tate,' Frost nodded. 'Where'd you find him?' he asked Lando.

'I overheard a conversation in the Alhambra. One of the gents asked if they had gotten rid of that deputy from Winona. The other one said that Mansir had a reason for wanting him kept alive, and they had stuck him into a toolshed behind the stable. After a while I sort of wandered over that way. There was only one man standing guard, and he is going to have a headache this morning.'

'They hardly noticed us when we left town,' Tate put in. 'Almost to a man everybody we passed was drunk.

Whiskey at the Alhambra seems to be free for the Mansir riders.'

'How'd you find me?' Frost asked. Clara was busy in the kitchen stirring something in a large blue mixing-bowl. She was not looking toward the men. Tate smiled, weakly. His long black mustache barely twitched with the expression.

'We were riding past the restaurant and met this woman — Irene? — and asked her if she had an idea where you might be. She told us that all she could think of was that you would have ridden over to your girlfriend's house, so we came on ahead and found your horse in the barn and dropped our heads to sleep out there. Come daylight, here we are.'

Frost had cringed at the word 'girlfriend' when Tate spoke it, and in the kitchen Clara, who had glanced their way at the appellation, had opened her mouth as if to speak before she returned to furiously whipping the hotcake batter she was making.

'You two are a pair of detectives,' Frost said. He was more interested in finding out, 'What do we do now?'

'What we need is more men,' Lando said, shifting his legs, 'that's obvious. Are there any in Climax who would stand with us, Frost?'

Frost shook his head — Waxy? Johnstone? Luke Waylon? These were not fighting men and if they hadn't already fled town they were probably making plans to do just that. 'Nobody I can think of,' he answered. 'Unless . . . '

'Don't hold back on us, Frost,' Tate said, leaning forward, his puffed eyes intent. His scabbed hands were clenched between his knees. 'We're all in this together now.' Lando's eyes also urged Frost to answer.

In the kitchen Clara had fired up the griddle. She was doing her duty as a hostess, preparing to feed the men with whatever she had, although it was little enough. Frost had noticed how light the flour bag she had been using was in her hands. Undoubtedly she was unwilling to go into town to even try to buy the basic necessities. Frost looked her way, seeing only her slender, rigid back and the tension in her body. He told the two deputies, 'The only man I'm friendly with who might have help to offer is Anson Weaver, the owner of the Liberty Bell. He told me he has thirty hands riding for him. The trouble is, boys, he's also had a lot of newcomers showing up from the south to deal with of late.'

'Mansir riders?' Lando asked, his eyebrows lowering.

'I wouldn't know. It seems likely. One of them called me a 'lawman' while he was trying to bash my brains out. I don't know why they would hole up on the Liberty Bell.'

'It's a good cover,' the more experienced Barrett Tate said. 'They know that the ranchers are looking for help at round-up. They could bide their time there until Mansir said that Climax had been taken over. Which it has now.'

'Unless Mansir wanted the Liberty

Bell too,' Lando pointed out.

'Why would he?' Frost asked.

'Someone is going to have to feed his army of outlaws,' Tate said, with a glance at Lando.

'Liberty Bell has the beef to do that. Do you know how much forty men can eat in a day?'

'I hadn't thought of that,' Frost said.

'You can bet Mansir has — the man does nothing half way.'

Frost was deep in thought. If that had been a part of the plan all along, Mansir must have contacted Liberty Bell with what seemed a reasonable offer first. Why start a war with thirty or so cowhands over the cattle when they could be purchased? Would Anson Weaver have agreed to supply the outlaws? No, Frost did not think so. Not even at the risk of having his land overrun by thieves and killers.

Would he have sold out? No, again. Anson had been firm when he told Frost that he would never sell to anyone. The ranch was Ada's legacy.

But Mansir could have made a deal with another man — Calvin Weaver, who only wanted to sell his portion of the ranch and get away from the Liberty Bell, whether he intended to attend an eastern medical school or not — which Frost had begun to doubt.

The details of the plan were not clear, but in broad outline Frost thought he finally understood what was happening in Climax, on the Liberty Bell. And that everyone he knew or might care for was about to be trampled under the hoofs of Charles Mansir's outlaw army.

Lando and Tate were both watching him, waiting for him to say something.

'I guess we'd better have a talk with Anson Weaver,' Frost said, rising to his feet.

'Breakfast is ready, boys!' Clara called out almost cheerfully from the kitchen. It was a tone of voice Frost had seldom heard from the woman. But then, maybe she liked Tate and Lando.

The three lawmen filled themselves

up with Clara's hot-cakes drenched in honey, and cups of black coffee. Frost ate guiltily for reasons he could not explain to himself. When they rose to leave, dabbing their lips and chins with napkins, Lando tried to thank Clara for the breakfast, but she waved his gratitude away with a flutter of her hands.

'Friends don't thank friends for sending them on their way nourished.'

She said nothing to Frost.

They retrieved their horses from the barn and started on their way toward town. When they hit Main Street they would turn east toward the Liberty Bell. There were still more uncertainties about this business than Frost could calculate. What if Anson refused? What if he were dead? Suppose the gunmen out there decided to stand and fight?

'Your girlfriend is the cheerful sort,' Lando said out of the blue. They were passing along the oak-lined path toward town, a light warm breeze stirring the leaves overhead.

'And she's generous with her cooking,' Tate chipped in. 'And it's mighty good cooking.'

'She's not my girlfriend,' Frost said sullenly. From the corner of his eye he caught Lando and Tate looking at each other.

'Sorry,' Lando said, 'things shouldn't be taken for granted, I suppose. But from the way she was looking after you from the doorway when we rode out — '

'She was watching all three of us ride away,' Frost said defensively, knowing that he wished deeply that things were as the men assumed between him and Clara.

'It's all right,' Lando apologized. 'Whatever you say, Giles. I learned long ago to never make a comment about a man's love life. Am I right, Tate?'

'That's always been my position,' Barrett Tate agreed. 'Whatever you say it's bound to be a mistake.'

'I was just trying to tell you — ' Frost began, but the jabbing finger that

163

Barrett Tate had lifted ended his explanation.

'We have company,' Lando muttered.

Three men with horses, two of them dismounted, stood blocking the road east. They all held rifles and wore scowling expressions.

'What are they doing there?' Frost asked.

'It seems that Mansir doesn't want anyone riding that way. Or in from that direction. Do you boys feel like going to shooting?'

'It's kind of early for me,' Tate said in a low voice. His battered face crinkled into a semblance of a smile.

'All right,' Lando replied. 'We'll brazen it out, but be ready if any of them makes a move to fire.'

Their horses kicked up puffs of dust as they approached the guards through the dry heat of morning. The breeze still blew, but did nothing to cool anyone. The men watching them appeared dusty, thirsty and more than a little bit hungover. One of the standing men, their leader, wore leather chaps although they were far from chaparral country. His boots were scuffed, his red shirt stained, the rifle in his hands as bright and clean as the day it had come off the Winchester assembly line.

'These are men who are serious about their work,' Frost heard Tate mutter. In fact he had recognized the man in front, Lucas Gere, as a man wanted out of Tascosa for bank robbery and assault on a woman. Tate kept his own face lowered as they approached the watchful men.

'Hold up there!' the one with the chaps said, holding up his hand.

'What in hell do you think we're going to do!' Lando yelled back, reining in fiercely. He swung down from his palomino, saying, 'Dewey Skinner wants to see you.'

'What about?' the hungover Mansir man demanded. He winced when he spoke. He and the battered Barrett Tate exchanged a glance. Maybe the outlaw thought that they had attended the same rough party the night before.

Lando braced himself in front of their leader. 'How would I know what about?' he asked sharply. 'I just know he sounded mad.'

'Dewey's always mad,' the tall man in chaps said, spitting to one side.

'He told us to watch this road,' the third man, Lucas Gere, said, removing his hat to scratch his head. 'What are we supposed to do about that?'

Lando's expression was one of exasperation. 'And what do you think we're doing out here, just avoiding sleep?' The man with the hangover smiled dimly. 'We're supposed to cover the road. You'd better get back and see what Skinner has in mind.'

'Do you think we're going on a raid?' Lucas Gere asked.

'He don't confide in me,' Lando answered.

'I hope not,' the man with the hangover mumbled. 'I won't be in shape for it for at least another day.'

'Go here, go there,' the man in chaps

said sourly, as he mounted his horse. 'That's the reason I deserted the army in the first place.'

'No it's not, Dale,' Gere kicked in. 'It was the difference in pay if you remember.'

All of them smiled except for Dale, their apparent leader. From the saddle Dale told Lando, 'Remember, no one in or out of town.'

'Yeah, we've got that much figured out,' Lando said in a cool voice. Frost and Barrett Tate swung down from their horses, unsheathing their rifles. With some muttering among them the three guards rode off in the direction of Climax, their dust trailing up through the oak trees along the road.

'I think they're pulling up, Lando,' Tate said as he watched the Mansir men slow on their ride along the road. 'They must have talked it over.'

'Swing aboard then, boys — we're on our way!'

Giles Frost hit leather and heeled his buckskin roughly. Fifty yards on he veered from the road so as not to expose himself to a direct shot as Lando and Tate turned their ponies in the opposite direction, but none of the rifles behind them opened up. As they grouped themselves again, Frost pointed out the direction of travel to Liberty Bell to Lando and Tate.

Returning to the Liberty Bell was not the cheeriest of notions to Frost, but that was the course of action they had agreed upon. The day was bright, the wind fitful as they again reached the head of the trail leading down to Liberty Bell Ranch. Amazingly, Frost was feeling almost no pain this morning. He had a fear of a headache striking him when least expected, but that had not happened yet. Perhaps he had beaten it.

Nearing the ranch some four hours later, Lando called a halt on the side of the road where a single live oak tree stood in the shaded, sheltering curve of a granite bluff.

'How's everyone doing?' Lando asked, after taking a swig from his canteen.

'Not bad,' Tate replied, although if someone were watching the deputy closely, he would see that the beating Tate had taken had left him stiff and clumsy in his movements.

Frost nodded, 'I'm much better than I'd have thought.'

'Fine,' Tate said. 'You know we got lucky back there with the guards. I was half-expecting it to go to shooting.' He paused, looking eastward toward Liberty Bell. The long grasslands beyond the house could be plainly seen from where they rested, along with the tiny dark forms of the grazing cattle, now bunched to keep them from straying in preparation for round-up.

Tate told them, 'I'm thinking we should go in wearing badges. We might as well announce our presence — it might even convince a few of the more nervous Mansir riders to try slipping away. Every one of them probably has some sort of warrant on him from down his backtrail.'

'I suppose so,' Tate said. 'We'll be

marked men anyway once we go have a talk with Anson Weaver. Let every man think that he might be the one we're after.'

With that Lando slipped his deputy's badge from inside his vest and refastened it and Barrett Tate did the same. Then Tate leaned back and reached into his saddle-bags, tossing a spare badge to Frost, who caught it neatly.

'I wouldn't want you to feel naked, Deputy Frost,' Tate said.

★   ★   ★

When the three men approached the Weaver house, the sun was glinting off their silver stars, clear to anyone who might have been watching them. And there were a few. Frost noticed a pair of men standing near the barn who slipped back behind it, one man tugging the other's arm.

Lando had noticed it too. 'The rats will run,' he said. 'but watch out for back-shooters.'

Riding under the oaks which stood dark and stolid in the bright sunlight, only the leaves at the very tips of their branches trembling in the dry breeze, they approached the Liberty Bell ranch house. The ride had been long, and now Frost could feel the aches and pains of his body returning. Tate must have been feeling the same, for his face was drawn, his knuckles white where his hand was clenched over-tightly around the reins of his dun horse.

Frost could hear steel against iron in the smith's shed. Banger was hard at work this afternoon. A window parted in the front of the house and Frost had a quick glimpse of Fat Boy's face. As the three men swung down from their saddles, the front door opened and there stood Ada Weaver — perfect in a pale-blue dress, her blonde hair pinned up, the slightest dab of rouge on her cheeks and a smile on her lips.

'My God, Frost,' Lando said, 'another one?' Then to Barrett Tate he said, 'There's more to this boy than meets the eye.'

'Shut up,' Frost muttered.

As they stepped up onto the porch, Ada cried out, 'Giles! I thought I'd never see you again,' and came forward, her arms outstretched. She placed them around his waist and briefly held him tight.

'Well, they say the world travels in circles,' Giles said, now flushed from the brief hug Ada had given him in front of the other deputies.

'You didn't make it to Bisbee, then?' Ada asked, stepping back, smiling a perfunctory greeting to the other men, noting the badges all three wore.

'No, things sort of got turned around,' Frost answered. 'I'll tell you about it later. Right now we need to speak with your father. Is he up?'

Ada's face fell. Her smile slipped away. 'He doesn't get up any more, Giles. He might be awake. I'll send Fat Boy to see. Come in, you men must be hungry. I'll have Renee make you some dinner.'

'Maybe later,' Lando replied as they

stepped into the house. 'We really do need to talk to Mr Weaver first.'

Ada said, 'Maybe you should let Giles take care of that by himself. I'm afraid the sight of the three of you might be too much excitement for Father just now.'

Lando shrugged. He couldn't see how three instead of one would make that much difference, but he was a guest here and did not know the old man's situation. 'In that case, we'd appreciate some coffee and maybe a little bread to gnaw on while Frost visits with Mr Weaver.'

'On the Liberty Bell?' Ada said, looking vaguely insulted. 'You will not, you'll at least have roast beef sandwiches. We butcher a steer a day out here, you know. And they don't object at all to being eaten once they've been killed.'

Smiling pleasantly, Ada led the two deputies off toward the kitchen where Renee could be seen going about her daily tasks. Frost removed his hat and, holding it in his hands, took a deep, slow breath and mounted the stairs toward Anson Weaver's bedroom.

They needed help to save Climax, and Anson Weaver was the only one who could supply that help. If he was willing. It was the busiest time of year on the Liberty Bell and any attempt to aid the people of Climax would cost him time and manpower. Yet if he would not agree to help them, then there was only one possible outcome: Climax was doomed.

10

At the top of the carpeted stairs, Frost hesitated. From behind the door leading to Anson Weaver's bedroom he could hear the soft fluttering of snoring followed by a fit of horrible coughing. Anson might be asleep, but it could not be a comfortable sleep. Stepping forward, his hat in both hands, Frost knocked tentatively on the door. If the old man were truly asleep, he vowed he would leave him to whatever rest he could be getting.

Instead, as soon as his knuckles rapped on wood, there was a faint answering voice from within.

'Come in,' Anson Weaver called out hoarsely, and Frost swung the door open and stepped into the close confines of the room.

There was the mustiness of all sickrooms permeating the air. A yellow shade covered the only window there, and the pale light beaming through it cast Weaver's face to a sickly parchment-yellow. The rancher seemed to have withered away in the short time Frost had been gone.

'Who is it?' Weaver asked, for he had not opened his eyes, possibly in deference to the yellow sunlight.

'It's Giles Frost, Mr Weaver,' Frost said, moving closer to the bed, watching the blue-veined, claw-like hands of Weaver with their outsized knuckles working against the stained white comforter which had been thrown over him.

'Giles!' Weaver said with evident pleasure. 'I never thought we'd see you again on the Liberty Bell. Did you make it to Bisbee, then?'

'No, sir. I'm afraid I got sidetracked.'

'The usual course of one's life,' Weaver said. His eyes were open now, pale and milky. He struggled to lift himself enough to arrange a bolstering pillow behind him. Frost did not offer to help, not knowing how the gesture would be taken.

When Weaver had settled himself again, and following another spate of coughing during which Frost saw the blood from his lungs staining a handkerchief, many of which were stacked on a bedside table, the old man pointed, having noticed the star on Frost's dark-blue shirt front.

'Get your job back, did you?'

'No, sir. As you can see, this is a deputy sheriff's star. It's all part of that sidetrack I told you I got shuttled onto.'

'Do you feel like talking about it, Giles?'

'I almost have to,' Frost replied, 'if you're up to listening.'

''Course I am!' Weaver snapped back with an artificial strength. 'Sit down and tell me what's happened and what's brought you back.'

Frost settled into a straight-backed wooden chair at Weaver's bedside, his hat on his lap, and told the story as succinctly as he could. Weaver didn't need every small detail of the events. When he had finished giving Weaver the background, Frost said carefully, 'So I suppose you can see why we've ridden out here to talk to you.'

Anson Weaver wore a sagging frown. 'I see, but what am I to do, Giles? You know I need all of my men at round-up time.'

'Anyone who goes with us wouldn't be gone for more than a couple of days.'

'Those who are able to come back at all, you mean,' Weaver said, his eyes more alert now. He paused to cough again. Frost waited.

'There's an element of danger,' Frost had to admit. 'If we could we'd ride into Climax with a posse of lawfully deputized men . . . there just aren't that many men around. Except on the Liberty Bell.'

'I know that,' Weaver said. He was a little cross, obviously, but still pondering the situation. He was wise enough to know that not only Climax but his own ranch was threatened by the proximity of Charles Mansir's army of outlaws. He sighed wearily, coughed and let his fading eyes meet Frost's. His decision came rapidly. 'I can't order any man to ride with you, not under the circumstances you are describing. Find Martin Campbell and explain things as well as you can. Tell him I have agreed to let you take any man who is willing to go. Knowing my crew, there are more than a few knuckleheads who would be willing to go along just to get away from their daily routine and shoot their guns off. Giles, make sure they know what kind of men they will be facing in Mansir's outlaw crew.'

'I will, and I thank you, sir,' Giles Frost said. Weaver just waved his thanks away.

'The next time I promise to repay a man for a favor given, I'll put more thought into it beforehand,' the owner of the Liberty Bell said with a grunt. Frost grinned and rose from the chair. Before he had reached the door, Weaver said, 'You'd better tell Ada what's happening.'

'And Calvin — is he around?' Frost asked, and the old man's eyes went cold before he let his eyelids drop.

'I haven't seen Calvin for a while. Giles, please tell Fat Boy to come up here, will you? It seems suddenly to be time for a short glass of whiskey.'

Frost went out, unnecessarily trying to make no noise as he closed the door. He stopped and breathed deeply. He had gotten what he needed from the visit, but there was no way he could feel good about having made it. He had the normal aversion to visiting death beds, and felt that he had extracted a promise from a man who might normally have felt otherwise about making it.

He happened to pass Fat Boy in the broad living room and passed on Weaver's message to him. The bright-eyed servant shook his head; a sign of silent sorrow.

In the kitchen he found Ada leaning against a low pine counter, her arms crossed as Lando and Barrett Tate sat at the table with empty, crumb-filled plates before them, coffee cups in their hands. Renee was busy stirring and tasting something in a huge black kettle hanging from a chain in the kitchen fireplace. Beef stew, Frost guessed by the smell and the habits of the house.

'Well?' Lando asked, as soon as Frost had entered the room.

'He says we can go ahead with things — after we talk to the foreman.' He asked Ada, 'Do you know where Martin Campbell might be found?'

Her lips formed a small pout. 'No, I don't think I've seen him at all today. He could be anywhere. Why do you need him?'

Frost sat at the rough table. Renee brought him a clean cup and filled all three men's mugs with hot, dark coffee. Lando and Tate held their silence while Giles Frost explained matters to Ada the best he could. Her expression was not one of pleasure as she listened.

'Use our men to save Climax! I don't like the sound of that very much,' Ada said with concern. 'Why should we?'

She was against the idea and had every right to be. It was round-up time and they had already had difficulty finding good men to help out. For the Liberty Bell it was the once-a-year opportunity to get fat off beef sales or, alternatively, to wither up and maybe perish if the cattle couldn't be driven to market.

'It may be that a simple show of force will cause Mansir to rethink his plans and pull out,' Tate said, speaking up. He was looking much better now. He had been supplied with a clean shirt and a chance to wash up while Frost was upstairs.

Ada's eyes sparked a little as she switched her sharp gaze to Barrett Tate. 'And it may be that it won't,' Ada said. 'Not if he's half as tough as you all seem to think.'

'It may be not,' Tate mumbled since he could not argue with the woman's logic. None of the three deputies believed it either. Mansir had too much invested in Climax and the Liberty Bell now. He would fight the law tooth and nail.

'Has he, or anyone else, approached you about selling the Liberty Bell, Ada?' Frost wondered.

'Me? Of course not. And Father would never entertain the idea. As for Calvin . . . ' She shook her head and half-turned away. 'No, no one has ever approached me about selling the ranch.'

'You see, miss,' Lando put in quietly, cradling his coffee cup in both hands, 'Mansir won't want this herd ever to be started on a trail drive. He'll need them right where they are to provide beef for his army for what he hopes will be months to come while they ride out and raid the country around us, hit the railroad and the banks in small towns — and some not so small.

'I'm saying,' Lando told Ada, whose back was now turned to the table as she looked out the kitchen window at the familiar sight of her yard, 'Liberty Bell is going to have to fight Mansir one way or another, now or later. Your best chance is to help us out now while the gang remains at a smaller size, because, believe me, it will just grow and grow . . . '

'Oh!' Ada said in frustration, throwing her hands in the air. 'Do whatever you want, whatever my father has agreed to. I don't care any more!' With that she rushed out of the room, all eyes following her.

'Sorry about that,' Lando apologized.

'You were only speaking the truth,' Giles Frost said, reaching for his hat. 'Let's go see if we can find the foreman, shall we?'

Their three horses, hitched in the front of the house, still looked fresh, although they must be at least a little trail-weary. Frost's buckskin and Tate's stolid dun allowed them to mount without antics. Lando's palomino tossed its head and seemed ready and eager to run. Lando patted its neck, calming the animal a little. 'He's still young,' Lando told them. 'Which way, Frost?'

'Let's swing by the barn first. The farrier is working — I heard him at his anvil earlier. He might know where

Campbell planned to ride this morning.'

Starting that way, Tate lifted a pointing finger at a group of men riding away from the ranch in a southerly direction. 'We've frightened a few more off,' he said.

'Well and good, unless they're riding directly to Climax,' Lando commented.

'Which they well could be,' Tate said.

At a hail, Banger emerged from the barn, wearing his leather apron, wiping his blackened hands on a blue neckerchief. In answer to their question, the smith replied, 'Campbell went up-range, to help the boys look for strays in Panther Gap, but he'll be in early. His horse is about to throw that same shoe again. I keep telling him to ride around rocks, not over them, but you try to tell Martin Campbell anything and — '

Lando interrupted Banger. 'Soon, you say? Do you think we have time to feed our horses before he gets back?'

'I'd guess that you have the time. I'm not sure, though. You ask Martin

Campbell anything and — '

'Can you help us find the feed, Frost?'

Banger seemed to notice that Giles Frost was among the deputies for the first time. He stared at the badge. 'I didn't know you was back, Frost. I hardly recognized you. I didn't expect to see you again — not wearing a badge.'

'I know,' Giles said, 'but here I am.'

'I'd better get back before my forge blows cold, men. Oat bags are stacked in the back shed, fresh hay's in the loft. Help yourselves to whatever you need.'

After the horses had been quartered and fed the three deputies sat down to rest on whatever was available. Frost perched on a nail keg positioned near the barn door. Lando and Tate sat together on a wooden bench that had been constructed for cowboys to sit on while they waited for Banger to work on their horses. The steady ring of Banger's hammer against the anvil provided a not-unpleasant background to their thoughts.

Frost knew that Tate and Lando were trying to devise a plan for attacking Climax — both looked frustrated with the result. Frost, too, had been considering a plan for what must be done, but neither had his thoughts gotten far. In addition he was thinking about Ada, Anson Weaver and the fate of the Liberty Bell which might have taken in a wandering hobo only to have him turn and try to destroy the ranch. He also wondered: *where was Calvin Weaver*, and what was he up to? Could he be traitorously planning against his father's wishes to sell the ranch, or undermine the upcoming trail drive? Why would he? Simply because if he had desire to leave the ranch, be it to attend medical school or out of just plain restlessness, the half of the ranch his father had given him would not bring enough at sale to provide for all of his needs — if it could be sold at all, with what Calvin saw as reasonable alacrity. Perhaps he was so indifferent to his own sister's needs that he would look to sell the land whole. Bartering away the herd, or selling their graze, would ruin the Liberty Bell, if either was his plan.

Frost could not guess. Except he knew he had seen Calvin Weaver riding into Climax last night. And what sort of business could he have there other than meeting with someone important to his game, like Charles Mansir?

Banger placed his hammer down and, wiping his hands again, walked to the door. Frost had heard nothing, seen nothing and he asked the blacksmith, 'What is it?'

'Can't you hear it — a horse with a loose shoe walking.' Banger had extraordinary hearing when it came to horses and their gear, it seemed, for only now did Frost pick out the sounds of horses approaching.

'It'll be Campbell — wait and see. How someone who's been a horseman all his life could put this off, I can't say. One day he's going to ruin that sorrel.

Ride 'em and swap 'em if they go lame, that's what these cowboys think,' Banger continued to grumble to himself. Frost had risen to stand beside Banger, looking to the south as the farrier was.

'Who's that with him?' Frost asked, for now he could clearly make out two distant riders.

'Why, that's Calvin Weaver,' Banger answered with disapproving surprise. 'Don't you know horses at all?'

'I just didn't recognize it,' Frost said, slightly irritated, but Banger needed to keep his pride in his single area of expertise and so Frost added nothing more.

'We'd better have our talk with Campbell now,' Lando said as the two men drew nearer.

'And with young Weaver,' Tate said.

'The old man didn't specify that, did he, Frost?' Lando glanced at Frost for confirmation. 'We'll talk with the foreman first — if he wants to share the information with Calvin Weaver, well, that's his choice.'

'Anson Weaver is not real trusting of his son right now,' Giles Frost commented. 'At least, that's the feeling I was getting.'

'Like I said, then,' Lando growled, 'we talk to Campbell right now. If he has any doubt about matters then I guess he can go over to the house and confirm the decision with the old man.'

As Banger approached the incoming riders, berating Martin Campbell for riding a three-legged horse, Calvin Weaver remained mounted, his dark eyes studying the three deputies. 'What's all this?' he asked, as Frost separated himself from the others and walked to the gray horse where Calvin was perched, one foot free of the stirrup as if he were undecided whether to dismount or not.

'I can give you the short version,' Frost said to the unhappy-looking Calvin Weaver, and he told him why they had come and what his father had decided.

'The old fool,' Calvin Weaver muttered. 'We'll need any men we have to protect the herd and the range if any of this is true.'

'There's time enough to do both,' Frost said. 'We just think it's a better idea to hit Mansir while his men are all collected in one place.'

'In Climax,' Weaver spat.

'That's right.'

'That's why you came back, isn't it, *former* Marshal Frost? To save that fleabox of a town from destruction. Let me ask you this — what makes Climax worth the saving?'

Frost considered that briefly, found he had no real answer for Calvin's question and walked away after saying, 'They just want to stop Mansir — it's county business, not mine. Ask one of the regular deputies if you want to know more.'

Martin Campbell, after giving his horse over to Banger, stood listening to Lando and Tate, alternately nodding and shaking his head, obviously a little baffled and overwhelmed by this sudden turn in his daily routine as foreman and range captain. Was he expected now to lead a charge of untrained cowboys into Climax?

Lando was encouraging, Tate cajoling. Calvin Weaver sat his pony, lips tightly compressed — the man liked none of this, obviously. Was that because he was secretly in cahoots with Mansir, or because he feared for the Liberty Bell with so many men soon to be stripped from its defensive flanks?

'Give me five minutes with Anson Weaver,' Frost heard Campbell say. Then the foreman started off on foot toward the main house, his face expressionless, but drawn.

'What do we do now?' Frost asked Barrett Tate.

'Saddle our ponies, because one way or the other, we're riding.'

Banger's hammer began its chiming again as the unsaddled sorrel belonging to Martin Campbell stood patiently at hand. Perhaps the sorrel like some women was used to shopping frequently for new shoes.

By the time Frost had finished preparing the buckskin for whatever was to come, Campbell returned with his face grim but determined. 'There's no easy way to do this,' he told the deputies. 'I'd rather have held a bunkhouse meeting tonight, but I'm going to ride out to the range and ask each man I meet if he's in the mood for a bloody holiday. Banger! Is it all right if I take the black mare?'

'You're the boss,' Banger shrugged, looking up from his forge. He added, 'But try not to ride her over every pile of rocks you might come across!'

Tate observed, 'Those men who are willing to ride with us won't be in for at least an hour or two. By the time they equip themselves and switch horses if they think they need to, we'll be approaching sundown.'

'That might be the best time to hit Climax,' the optimistic Orlando Marsh said. 'Every Mansir man will likely be half-drunk, and we'll be among the shadows.'

'There's the guards posted on the east end of town,' Frost reminded them. 'If they see us approaching, they'll raise a ruckus and send a man racing to town to warn Mansir.'

'All right,' Tate said thoughtfully, sucking at one end of his black mustache. 'We'll take care of those guards first. Do you want the job, Frost? Pick a few men and clear the way for our little army?'

Lando was watching Frost as he considered. 'A little gun-shy now, are you, Frost?'

'You'd be, too, if you'd been dusted with bullets as often as I have been lately. But if you're asking me will I do it, the answer is yes. There's going to be shooting everywhere on this night. When I take my first bullet makes no difference. I'll ask Campbell who his most seasoned men are, and pick three.'

With their plan, such as it was, in place, the three deputies again seated themselves and waited as the cowboys off the Liberty Bell Ranch, those who had volunteered to ride to Climax, straggled in singly or in pairs. Some of these wanted to change mounts, others had determined that their familiar cow ponies were in good enough shape to carry them the distance to Climax. Many of the men had stopped off at the bunkhouse to collect more ammunition than they normally carried on ranch duties.

There was a variety of men reporting. Most seemed to be a young, fresh-faced, bantering crew eager with the excitement of battle. A few were weather-scoured, taciturn veterans who saw to exchanging horses and loading their gear without speaking, without complaining. They worked for Anson Weaver and the Liberty Bell, and whatever was required, they were willing to give.

Even their lives.

11

They trailed out toward Climax as the sun began to heel low over the mountains and the shadows across the land grew long. The buckskin, fed, watered and refreshed, moved easily under Frost. The other riders stretched out behind him. The younger men had now stopped their calling, cheering and bantering as the reality of what they were about to attempt sank in. As they met the foothills and began to ascend, Frost noticed that Calvin Weaver rode on steadily with them. Why Calvin had decided to come was anyone's guess, the most likely being that he was trying to please his father, but really there was no knowing.

Calvin Weaver rode to the right of and slightly behind Frost, who slowed his buckskin and allowed Calvin to come alongside. He had been wanting to talk to Anson's son and now seemed as good a time as ever. Young Weaver's eyes were hidden in the shadow of his tugged-down hat brim, but his mouth gave away his displeasure at Frost's approach.

'Long trail,' Frost tried.

'And no good at its end,' Calvin answered.

'Why are you riding with us, then?' Frost enquired.

'Why? Look, Frost, Climax is your town — or was — but the Liberty Bell is my ranch — or will be. What you men were saying was the truth. We have a chance to stop Mansir now, and if we don't, the battle will shift to home range. I don't like the idea of fighting in my own backyard.'

They rode silently for a while, picking their way along the slope toward where it met the road into Climax. At the top of the rise where they all halted to let their ponies breathe, Frost commented, 'You've met Charles Mansir, I take it.'

Calvin Weaver seemed to stiffen

slightly in his saddle. 'I don't know what led you to that conclusion, but as a matter of fact, you're right. I have met the man.'

'And . . . ?' Frost prompted.

Weaver's answering voice was a whiplash. 'And *what*? What is it you want from me, Frost?'

'The truth. I like to know who I'm riding with.'

Calvin tilted back his hat. Late reddish sunlight flushed his face. 'I didn't want to talk about it,' Weaver said, 'not to you and certainly not to my father. But it seems it's all going to come out anyway. My sister has been talking to Mansir's emissary.'

'Dewey Skinner?'

'How did you know that? Never mind. Yes, Skinner. He told her what Mansir proposed — to buy the Liberty Bell and all the cattle standing on it. In one payment! That takes a lot of cash, as you can imagine, Frost, but Mansir's got it from raiding this territory for years. Ada said she didn't dare as long as Father was alive, but promised him that as soon as he was gone — which seems to be imminent — and I was gone east with a fair amount of money given to me by Mansir or some confederate in a mock purchase of my sections of the ranch, she would entertain his proposal. She believes this country is no place for a young woman.'

'May I ask how you found out about all of this?' Frost asked, uncertain whether he believed the man or not.

'I had my suspicions, so I went to talk to Mansir himself. What an oily, cocksure man he is. I told him that Ada had given me a few indications that there might be a buyer for the Liberty Bell and I needed to know if it was true and what was in it for me. He told me the entire plan and mentioned an extraordinary number for my share of the Liberty Bell.'

That was the night Frost had seen the young man riding into Climax. It must have taken a lot of nerve for Calvin to ride into town alone . . . if any of this were true.

'I can't believe that Ada would — '

'You don't know Ada at all!' Calvin snapped. 'She's skilled at presenting herself as cheerful, caring, tender even — but she has the Devil himself in her. You can take my word for it; I've known her all my life, and she is not what she seems to the casual visitor.'

Tate had decided that the horses had had enough rest and they began to move on toward Climax again. Again Calvin let his horse trail off to the right and lag a little bit. The man obviously wanted to be alone. Frost tugged his hat lower against the fading sun and rode on.

Now Climax could be seen in the distance, the buildings as small as matchboxes, and Frost drifted over to where Tate and Lando rode in a group with Martin Campbell. He nodded to Lando and asked Tate, 'It's getting to be that time. What do I do and who's going with me?'

'We've been discussing that. We assume

200

that the three guards posted along the road are still in the same position. It's best if you can take them without a huge uproar, although with the constant, aimless firing of guns in Climax, several more shots aren't likely to spark much interest. Taking our whole army up to them will surely spook them. You three or four — however many men you think it will take — should just approach them as any other men seeking to enlist in the outlaw army. They've seen you before, but I doubt anyone will recognize you, and the guard has undoubtedly changed since we met Dale and Lucas Gere standing watch along the road.

'Probably it's best to have a couple of men circle in from the north and south to surprise their flanks. Then . . . it might go against the grain, but try to get off the first shots. The rest of us are depending on you.'

'Any suggestions as to who I should take with me?' Frost asked, looking now at Martin Campbell, whose face was grim. These were his riders, his friends he was taking into battle.

'We can't afford to let this be fouled up by anyone trigger-happy or shy,' Campbell answered, as if he had already given the matter long thought. 'Take Derik Barnes and Smokey Chalmers. I'll pass the word on to them. If you need a fourth, and you probably will, I'll ask Rome Fletcher if he'll ride with you. Fletcher is a former cavalry officer and hard to get along with only because he's used to being in charge, but he has a sure eye and nerves of steel.'

'All right. I'll take your recommendations — you know the men and I don't After this next hillrise, it will be time for us to drop down toward the flats. I need to meet with them now,' Frost said. He could feel his own brow trickling sweat and it was not from the heat of the evening. Could what Lando had suggested earlier be the truth? Was he gun-shy — so shaky about being hit again that he was no use as a lawman now, when he would be forced to exchange bullets with the guards posted along the road?

Giles Frost's head began to throb with a sort of anxious warning. He forced himself to calm and consider what he had always done for a living, even if maintaining the law in Climax had not involved much in the way of gunplay. He was a lawman.

Martin Campbell was returning through the dusky light, trailed by three hard-bitten men whom he introduced to Frost as they rode briefly in a tight knot. Derik Barnes was a bulky man with a scar on his left cheek as if he had once been a duelist. Smokey Chalmers had a thatch of blond hair which escaped from his hat and blew across his eyes. The mustache he wore had gone gray, indicating that he had seen a few years pass by. In fact, Frost decided, he himself was the youngest of the group. Whether that was for the better or worse, he did not know. Rome Fletcher, the former cavalry officer, had steely-gray eyes with weather-cut wrinkles spraying out from the corners, a lean, hard, tanned face and a gaze that seemed to look straight through a man.

Frost told them what they had decided to do. 'Two of us — let's make it Barnes and Chalmers — will approach the checkpoint from the north and south. Whoever takes the north will have to get riding soon to find his position.'

Smokey Chalmers lifted a gloved hand. 'I'll take that job,' he volunteered.

'Fine, Barnes, that leaves you to come up on the southern flank. There isn't much in the way of cover on this side, but it's growing dark and if you can slip down one of the feeder canyons along the way, you should be able to come upon them unseen.'

'That leaves you and me,' Rome Fletcher said, his hard eyes studying Frost closely. 'We ride straight up to the guards, do we?'

'That's the idea. We're two tough *hombres* from somewhere, meaning to join up with Mansir's army.'

'Santa Fe,' Rome Fletcher said.

'What?' Frost said, not getting his point.

'We're up from Santa Fe where we rode with Lou Boss and the Red Butte bunch. I know enough about Santa Fe and Lou Boss to talk my way through if someone asks any questions.'

'All right,' Frost agreed, but he added, 'men — I doubt that this is going to go on long enough for any of us to have a conversation. Shoot first and shoot straight; we don't want it to sound like an army's approaching.'

That was easy enough to say, and the plan was simplicity itself. The question was, would it work? Not many plans in a man's life ended up as expected.

As night continued to fall, Tate, Lando and the Liberty Bell bunch continued to plod on, heading straight for Climax. Chalmers and Barnes had already broken off to find their own ways through the near-darkness toward the spot where Mansir's men had set up their checkpoint. After those two were well on their way, Frost nodded to Rome Fletcher and they too broke away from the main party of men and dipped down toward the road leading into town. Neither man spoke along the way. There was nothing useful that could be said. Fletcher had checked the loads in his two handguns and his Winchester and Frost followed suit. They were as ready as they were going to get, although it was not nearly ready enough. Frost glanced to the north where heavy timber grew and to the south where the rocky hills launched themselves against the purpling sky, but he could not make out so much as a shadow indicating where Smokey Chalmers and Derik Barnes might be. But that was the way it was supposed to be. Frost could only hope that their timing was co-ordinated well enough so that they met up at the checkpoint and all hands were ready to enter the battle together.

Behind them the Liberty Bell soldiers were arriving, holding back a little, waiting for the checkpoint to be breached.

There was no way of predicting how matters would unfold at the checkpoint, no way of knowing how things would eventuate in Climax. All that was certain as Frost and Rome Fletcher continued along their twilight journey was that the battle for Climax had been entered and blood would be shed, men's lives lost.

Charles Mansir was not going to enjoy this night in the least.

In the twilight glow, the shadows of the men standing watch on the road resembled stick figures as Rome Fletcher and Frost approached. The three guards were all afoot, their horses tethered in the trees beside the trail. Giles Frost was uneasy, his mouth dry. This might be war, but he had a strong aversion to shooting down unknown men where they stood, even knowing that they might have the same treatment in mind for him.

'Ho! What's all this — an armed camp?' Rome Fletcher called out when they were within fifty feet of the waiting guards.

'That's what it is,' the bulkier of the three watching guards answered, stepping toward them with his rifle in both hands. 'Who the hell are you?'

'Traveling soldiers,' Fletcher replied. 'We were told that Mansir was hiring on.'

'Might be that he is,' the guard said, 'but he's kind of choosy about who he hires.' The guard came three steps nearer. 'I can't make out your faces. Who'd you say you were?'

There was movement in the shadows off to their left and a small rolling sound. Barnes, if it was him, must have dislodged some rocks on his way down the slope. As the three men whirled that way a Winchester from the timber to the north opened up. Smokey Chalmers had found his position.

And he had found his range. One of the three men standing guard threw up his hands, dropping his rifle as he folded up and fell to the ground. The bulky man in front of them cursed violently and shouldered his rifle, aiming it at Frost. There was firing from the south and from Rome Fletcher's pistol beside him. Frost heard it all but saw none of it. His head exploded with brilliant yellow light and he was tumbling to the ground, the world going crimson and then black.

When he found himself able to see again, to sit up on the hard, cold ground, he was surrounded by men: Martin Campbell, Smokey Chalmers, Tate and Lando.

'He's coming around,' a muffled voice announced.

'I can't find a bullet wound,' someone else said.

'I told you he was never hit,' Rome Fletcher said with heated anger. 'He just bailed out of the saddle when they started shooting at us.'

Lando was bent over Frost. Now he extended a hand to assist Frost to his feet. 'What happened, Giles?' the deputy asked.

'One of those damned headaches. Everything went black — just when they needed me.'

'It looks like they didn't need you that much,' Lando said, indicating the three dead men whose bodies had been tugged to the side of the road.

'But what do they think of me?' Giles Frost asked, trying to steady his trembling legs. 'That I'm gun-shy, a coward. You heard Rome.'

'Rome Fletcher knows nothing of you having been shot in the head a few days ago. I wouldn't bother trying to explain it. There's no time for that now, anyway.'

'On to Climax,' Frost muttered.

'That's right — on to Climax.'

They held a brief planning conference then. Rome Fletcher was all for storming the town, letting the chips fall where they may. Tate and Lando were more cautious in their thinking.

'We should try to disperse our men a little,' Tate was saying. 'Maybe we can be among them before they have time to react and fight back.'

Lando agreed. 'Filter in — a few to

the alley on the north side of town, others to the south.'

'Well, you're the men in charge,' Rome said. But the former army officer whose habit had always been to charge the enemy directly and overwhelm him with superior force was not happy with the strategy. 'They'll spot any number of men lurking around.'

'I have an idea,' Frost said, speaking up. As Rome turned his glare on him, Giles suggested, 'I say we send about four men riding in first, racing their horses at dead top speed right on through town. It's common to see horse races down Main Street at this time of night when the men are starting to get whiskey-exuberant.'

'Just ride straight through?' Tate repeated. 'It's kind of dangerous, isn't it?'

'I don't think so,' Giles replied. 'Besides, if anyone happens to get suspicious, the men will already be out of town and riding away fast.'

'Before anyone can identify them or

think of grabbing a gun and firing at them,' Tate said, nodding his understanding.

'Exactly. A few of your young bucks might be willing to try that gambit,' Frost said to Martin Campbell. 'If what you say is true they came along mostly for the sport of yahooing anyway.'

'I'm sure I can find more than a couple of men who would be up for it. They will see it as nothing more than a lark.'

Lando was catching on to the idea now. 'While they're causing a few minutes of commotion, we can slip our men into the back alleys — no one will be looking their way.'

'That's what I'm thinking,' Frost said.

'And we'll end up with four of our men on the other side of town when the shooting does break out,' Tate said, stroking his black mustache. 'I think it's worth a try, Frost.'

'I have a question,' Rome Fletcher put in. His piercing eyes were still fixed on Frost whom he now took for a coward. He was going to be against anything Giles suggested. 'We're talking about fifty, maybe a hundred armed men going at it with Colts and rifles. If we disperse our force, how's anyone going to know the enemy from his brother-at-arms in the darkness?'

'I've thought of that,' Giles said calmly. 'It might hurt some of the boys' feelings, but I suggest that none of us wears a hat. It's that simple.'

'There will be some of Mansir's men who might be hatless,' Rome argued.

Tate answered him. 'In this part of the country, Rome! How many men do you see riding around here without a hat? Most of 'em are as protective of their Stetsons as they are of their ponies.'

Rome grumbled a response which was no response. Campbell went off to tell his gathered cowboys what the plan was to be and to recruit three or four men who would be responsible for the diversion. These were picked by Campbell, given their instructions and told to remove their hats at the end of their ride. The rest of the cowhands could be seen stuffing their hats into their saddle-bags. Obviously they were not pleased. Riding without a hat was just a notch above riding around in long-johns to them. Nevertheless they complied. Campbell and Tate — who knew the town — laid out the plan for the other men, those who would be charged with filtering into Climax and concealing themselves.

'That only leaves you three lawmen,' Rome was saying to Lando. 'What is it you badge-toters have in mind for yourselves?'

'Obvious, isn't it?' Lando answered. 'We're going after Charles Mansir. We mean to cut off the head of the snake.'

12

As Martin Campbell gathered the Liberty Bell hands and discussed the roles they were expected to play in the assault on Climax, Frost waited impatiently. He had no fear at that moment but the fear of failure. He could not let Climax down no matter how shabbily he felt the town had treated him, nor Anson Weaver, who had trusted him enough to allow him to recruit his Liberty Bell cowboys for the retaking of the town. Nor ... Clara Finch. He thought of her again sharply, distinctly. He doubted that the young woman was in any immediate danger, but there was certainly danger surrounding her like a dark storm cloud about to erupt with lightning and thunder.

The other two deputies, Tate and Lando, were talking over their own plan as Frost walked his horse toward them.

'Anything I need to do?' Giles Frost asked.

'We've talked it over, Frost. Tate and I both feel that it's our job to go after Mansir. That's why we came to Climax, after all.'

'Where do you think he's hiding? Or is he hiding — not knowing that the sky is about to fall?'

'That's what I was trying to find out before I got jumped and landed in that shed where Lando found me,' Tate answered. 'He almost certainly is in one of the rooms above the Alhambra Saloon. Walking around it I looked for, and found, a back stairway leading up from the alley. The trouble was that there were two guards posted there, and these are the ones who caught me and roughed me up. One other thing I did notice before they hauled me away was that there's a sort of trip-wire stretched across the fourth step up. Oh, Mansir is watching himself, for sure, with that murder warrant out of Winona on him. And he knows that sheriff's deputies have already been there looking for him.'

'You'll need some help if he's that well forted up,' said Calvin Weaver, who had appeared out of nowhere.

'Maybe so, maybe not,' Tate said, eyeing the rancher's son. 'What makes it anything you'd want to get mixed up in?'

'He's trying to steal my entire life from me,' Calvin said. His tone was so serious and pleading at once, that the two deputies looked at each other and shrugged.

'All right, then. You ride with us, Weaver. Frost,' he added as an afterthought, 'you might as well come along too. If we're forced to switch plans and go in in force, maybe we can use one more gun.'

'Look no further,' Rome Fletcher, who had been sitting his horse on the periphery, spoke up. 'I'll join you.'

Tate frowned slightly at the old cavalry officer, whose manner had been only belligerent up to now. 'All right, but Deputy Lando and I are in charge,' Tate said. 'Do you understand?'

'I've given orders in my time, but I've also taken a few,' Rome answered. 'Now, how do we intend to approach the target?'

Barrett Tate sucked in a deep breath and slowly exhaled through pursed lips. This last-minute change in plans required some quick rethinking of the approach he and Lando had intended to try. Maybe they were better off with more guns on their side; Tate could not be sure.

'All right, we'll try it this way,' Tate told them. 'Lando and I will go up the back stairs as we had planned. Frost, we might need you along to help us with the guards posted there. After we're on our way up, you can stand watch there in case help tries to come up that way, or Mansir tries to flee in that direction.

'Weaver here, and Rome, can just walk into the saloon. They don't know Rome, and they've only seen Calvin a few times before, the last time meeting with Mansir himself. It's unlikely that anyone in that mob will even notice them at all.

'When the action starts outside, the saloon will empty out. There'll be a rush for the door, and maybe a few men will try to run upstairs — Rome and Calvin will move that way after them. Depending on the situation,' he said to Rome, 'just guard that end of the hallway, or come quick if you hear shooting.

'Does that make sense to everybody?' Lando asked.

'Not much,' Rome said unhappily, 'but if you are asking if it's clear to us, the answer is yes.'

Lando frowned in the darkness. Martin Campbell had returned with four very young-looking horsemen, probably none had yet seen his eighteenth birthday. 'Are these our racers?' Tate asked. The young men looked cocky sitting their ponies there as night began to settle. They were still too young to fear death.

'This is them. I told them to wear

their hats through town, pack them after they reached the end of Main Street.'

'That's it,' Tate said. 'Yahoo your way down the street, boys. If you want to let off a couple of shots in the air if you can, all the better. We want to grab attention.'

'Think we can't ride with one hand on the reins?' one of the youngsters asked in a voice that was almost taunting.

'I don't know and I don't care,' Barrett Tate said, 'just make sure you do your job. That little ride is going to be the fuse that lights a huge bomb.'

As the kids rode away, one of them snickering, Tate told Campbell, 'We're starting out now,' indicating the deputies, Rome and Calvin. 'We have to be in place before the ruckus begins.'

'I've got it,' Campbell said, 'though I can't guarantee any of this will work. By the way, I apologize for the kid. It seems there are a few things his pappy forgot to teach him.'

'No matter,' Tate said dismissively. 'It doesn't require an apology — not from you at least; you're not his pappy.'

They had other things of more concern than a youngster who had not yet learned his manners and had not yet apparently come to realize that this ride through town could be the last time he would sit a horse in this life.

Frost, the two deputies, Calvin Weaver and Rome started along the dark road toward the beacon of the riotously lighted town of Climax. Glancing back Frost could see Martin Campbell ordering his night riders for the assault on Climax.

The two deputies rode in front, followed by Frost and Rome. Calvin Weaver trailing, his dark face set and determined. From time to time Rome Fletcher glanced at Giles Frost, and Frost thought he knew what the old cavalryman was thinking: that Frost was not to be trusted when the chips were down, that he was gun-shy and likely a coward. Frost was uneasy as well, not because of Rome's disapprobation, but from fear that his malady, those blinding headaches, might recur at precisely the wrong moment.

It did no good to worry about that now. Reaching the head of the first cross-alley from where the wild, seemingly endless riotous celebrating of Mansir's outlaw camp could be seen, Tate turned and gestured to Frost and Lando and the three entered the relative quiet and coolness of the alley to try working their way behind the Alhambra where Charles Mansir was almost certainly forted up in some upstairs room. Which room, they could not even guess, and there could be a dozen gunmen hidden behind the doors along the corridor.

There were six rooms upstairs, Giles Frost knew. In the past five of them had been provided to the saloon girls who worked in the establishment, with only a single room at the head of the inside stairs being reserved for the occasional traveler passing through the town.

There was no reason to think that Toledo had had the time or motivation to alter the arrangement. Frost mentioned this to Tate and Lando as they rode, although the information was of no great value. The deputies would have to work their way along the corridor not knowing if each room contained one or more of Mansir's hired soldiers, or just a sleepy-eyed working girl.

Or both.

The night held silent, if the constant uproar in the saloon and in the street, the cursing, fighting, shooting could be called silence. There was no way of knowing how far Campbell had advanced his cowboy army into the dark alleys on either side of Main Street. By the time the three deputies had approached the back stairs of the Alhambra, there was still no sight of them. Frost had the idea that Campbell was holding them back until the race down the street by the wildly whooping Liberty Bell riders had begun.

Meanwhile, the alley behind the

Alhambra was a pocket of darkness swathed in a gloomy sort of silence. Two Mansir men guarded the foot of the outside steps leading to the sleeping area of the Alhambra. Tate held up a hand and whispered, 'All right, men, let's try it.'

Tate had decided that he and Lando would walk around the corner of the building, leading their horses, lifting a hand in a casual greeting as they passed by. The darkness and the bodies of their horses would keep them from being identified as anything but passing gang members. In the meantime, as the guards' eyes followed them along the side alley, Giles Frost was to creep up on the guards through the thickness of the shadows and get the drop on them. There was no guarantee, of course, but the hope was that the guards would be too surprised to turn and begin firing. Silence was desirable, but not to be relied upon. All that was certain was that these two men had to be removed so that the deputies could storm the

Alhambra's upper reaches and dig Mansir out of his lair.

It was then, with perfect timing, that the sounds of horses racing along Main Street could be heard. There was cat-calling and yahooing and pistols being fired into the air as Martin Campbell's young cowboys ran the length of the street on their ponies. Both of the guards glanced that way and one of them stepped out into the alley for a better look. When he returned, smiling and shaking his head, Giles Frost said silently from the shadows between the building and the stairs, 'Drop those guns, men, or you're surely dead.'

Both decided they would rather live to see tomorrow, and the rifles were discarded on the oily floor of the alleyway just as Tate and Lando returned, pistols in hand. Lando had taken a coil of rope from his horse's saddle and he proceeded to tie up the two men, who were too angry, too surprised to say anything, or offer any resistance. Tate stood over them with the muzzle of his pistol aimed at their heads as the men were bound at the ankles, their hands strapped behind their backs, their own scarves used as gags.

'You're two of the lucky ones,' Giles said, crouching down to test the knots in their hastily tied bonds. 'A lot of men are going to die this night. If you two just hold still until it's over and then work yourselves free, you'll survive. But, once you do manage to get free, I'd suggest that you hit leather and ride out of my town.'

Tate glanced his way as Frost said that: 'My town'. Why had he even called it that? It was not his, had not been for some time, and never would be again. He felt like saying as much to Tate and Lando, but the two deputies were already on their way up the wooden outside steps, Tate's last gesture indicated that Frost was to remain where he was and watch the entrance for any visitors who might show up — the

226

guards' relief or someone with business to conduct with Charles Mansir.

Along the back alley now Frost could hear slowly moving horses approaching his position. He slipped his pistol from its holster and with a glance at the two prisoners, peered into the alleyway. There was a group of Liberty Bell cowboys riding toward him. He could tell because none of the men wore a hat. Cursing himself silently, Frost remembered that he had not removed his own hat. Now he did and sent it sailing into the deeper shadows.

Mooncast shadows sketched the progress of the riders along the way. Frost whistled softly and stepped cautiously into the alley as the men drew nearer. He recognized the rider at the front of the group and whispered, 'Campbell!' Most of the men behind him had their Colts drawn or their rifles placed across their horses' withers, ready for combat.

'Hello, Frost,' the Liberty Bell foreman said, raising a hand to indicate to the men following him that everything was all right for the time being. 'What's happening?'

'Tate and Lando slipped upstairs. I haven't heard any commotion yet. It's pretty quiet along the street, too.'

'Good for us — we haven't gotten all our men in position yet, as you can see.'

'I'll let you get along then — ' Frost began, but abruptly there was the echoing sounds of heavy pistol fire from upstairs in the Alhambra Saloon. The rear door opened and a man rushed out onto the landing, holding his chest. He turned, fired back once into the hallway and then raced down the steps, taking them three at a time. He had forgotten, or didn't know about, the trip wire that had been strung there. His boot got tangled in it and the man threw up his hands, grasping at the sky. He turned a wild-eyed pale face toward them, then fell onto the steps. They could hear the ugly sound of his neck breaking as he hit the wood.

'Who is it?' Campbell wanted to

know. From out on the street now guns had opened up from various points along Main Street. Frost had gone to the body of the dead man, turning him over.

'It's Dewey Skinner,' he told Campbell, as more pistol shots racketed from upstairs in the Alhambra.

'Who the hell is — ?' Campbell tried to ask.

'Never mind. Can you have a couple of your men guard these prisoners and watch the staircase so that no one comes up behind us?'

'I suppose. What are you going to do?'

'Go up there,' Frost said, lifting his chin toward the Alhambra's second floor. 'From the sound of it, my friends might need a little help.'

Then without waiting for a reply, Frost hit the wooden steps, maneuvering around Dewey Skinner's fallen form, slipping neatly over the trip wire on the fourth riser, and rushed to the back door of the Alhambra, which stood open.

Inside the Alhambra it was like a war zone. Guns fired from every door and down the hallway. Black smoke clotted the air, stinging Frost's eyes and nostrils. Through the smoky cloud, he saw a dead, unknown outlaw sprawled against the corridor carpet, his gun flung from his hand, his eyes wide and sightless. Behind him in the doorway stood a young-old woman Frost knew as Sally, one of the regular saloon girls, in a pink silk wrapper, her hand to her painted lips, her eyes pleading with Frost.

'Anyone else in that room?' Frost rasped.

'No, Marshal,' was the shaky reply.

'Then get back in there, and stay there!'

Frost stepped over the body of the dead man and began working his way toward the head of the corridor, toward the guest room Toledo had previously reserved for the rare occasional visitor to Climax. Frost's guess seemed to have been right — that was where Charles

Mansir had decided to make his last stand.

A Colt .44 banged out, followed by a more-muffled answering shot. Tate and Lando seemed to be trying to breach the door, though Frost could not see them through the smoke. He passed a second downed gunman, but this one was not dead. He writhed on the floor, holding his belly, his tormented pleas pitiful.

'Get a doctor, Al! Get me to a doctor!'

Frost took a moment to crouch beside the man, slide his pistol away from his hand and tell him, 'We've got one on the way. Just hold on.'

From the room across the hall the door popped open like the lid on a jack-in-the-box and an arm appeared, silver pistol in hand. Frost hit the carpet and fired up from his back into the partially open doorway, drawing a bellow of pain from his attacker. The man, whoever he was, stumbled forward two steps, tried to fire at Frost, his bullet hitting the carpet, and Frost shot him again.

His own actions had added to the fog of black smoke in the corridor, and Frost still could not see the two deputies ahead nor assess their situation. He called out: 'Tate? Lando!'

'Who's there?' he heard Tate's voice call back.

'Frost! Can I come ahead?'

'Come on; be quick about it!'

Reaching the two lawmen he found Lando seated on the floor against the wall, holding his leg, which had been hit. There was a red gash across Tate's forehead as if he had come that close to taking a bullet to his brain.

'Anyone else around?' Frost asked. By now Rome and Calvin should have made it up the inside stairs leading from the saloon. Tate's voice was a pant as he answered. He was thumbing fresh loads into his revolver.

'They haven't shown. Maybe they were recognized downstairs after all.' His expression was grim. His dark hair was hanging down across his brow. His face was smoke-smudged. Beyond the walls they could hear a barrage of shots which sounded like they were fighting Gettysburg all over again in the streets of Climax.

'Did our boys make it in?' Tate asked, snapping the loading gate on his pistol shut.

'I saw Campbell. But I don't know if they had time to get set up before this started. As for the boys on the south side of town, who knows,' Frost shrugged. He pasted a thin smile on his lips and added, 'But someone is making one hell of a battle of it out there.'

Then he asked in a low voice, 'What's happening here?' He nodded toward the room where Mansir was supposedly forted up.

'There's at least three or four men with weapons holed up in there. When we arrived, Dewey Skinner burst out of there and started shooting. He creased my skull, but Lando shot him in the chest. Dewey ran down the hallway, trying to get help or to escape, I don't know which.'

'Skinner is out of it now,' Frost advised the deputy sheriff. 'He broke his neck trying to run down the outside stairs.' Or maybe it was Lando's bullet that had done the job — it made no difference.

Behind them now Rome and Calvin belatedly rushed up the inner stairs. 'Had to fight our way up,' Calvin panted. There was a heavy bruise on his forehead. Another shot from within the room punctured the door, sending a spray of lacquered splinters outward. Tate spun and without hesitation fired three rounds from his .44 into the room. A man groaned. They heard a shuffle of movement.

Rome stepped forward, wanting to be in the center of things. Behind the cavalry officer Frost saw a shadowy movement and a man, cocked revolver in his hand, came up the stairs behind Rome. Rome Fletcher turned that way at the sound of the approaching steps, but he was already in the outlaw's sights.

Frost raised his Colt and fired twice, and the gunman could be seen slipping and then tumbling down the interior stairs. Rome, pistol half out of his holster, watched the falling man and then turned back toward Frost.

'Thanks, Frost, I — '

Giles cut his apology off. 'Forget it, Rome. We're on the same side in this war.'

There was silence within the barricaded room now. Tate stood as near to it, listening, as he could safely do. Lando, still holding his bleeding leg, had begun to mutter a string of novel and vehement oaths.

Down the hallway where smoke still hung heavily, a door opened and someone peered out.

'Sally!' Frost called out. He held up a hand to her and then boosted Lando to his feet. 'Come on.' Helping the limping Lando along the hallway, he led the wounded deputy into Sally's room.

Beyond the window a full-scale battle for Climax was still going on between the Liberty Bell riders and the outlaws.

'Can you help out the deputy, Sally?' Frost asked, still propping up the injured Lando, whose face was twisted with anguish.

'Can I?' Sally said with excitement. 'Marshal, I'll do anything I can to help out the law.' She helped lower Lando to a sitting position on her unmade bed. 'This last week in Climax, since you went away, has been . . . '

Frost didn't listen to the rest. He could guess how it had been in Climax. At the end of the hall Tate and the others still held themselves away from the door. Frost asked Barrett Tate, 'What do you want to do? We can't just stand here and wait.'

'I know it,' Tate muttered from behind his drooping black mustache. 'All right, boys, watch my back — I'm going in.' The deputy sheriff shot the lock off the door, kicked the already battered piece of wood and rolled in, raising his gun in anticipation. The window to the hotel room was open wide, the flimsy curtains fluttering in the night breeze. In one corner of the room, slumped to the floor near the foot of the bed, sat a single man. Tate and Frost recognized him immediately: it was Lucas Gere, the outlaw wanted for abducting a woman and for murder. Gere's face was ashen. On his red shirt front was a tell-tale blot of maroon. He held one arm limply. His gun had been tossed aside on the wooden floor.

'Hello, Tate,' the gunman said with a pain-twisted smile. 'Finally got me, did you?'

'It's not you I'm looking for — where's Charles Mansir?'

'He's gone,' Gere told them, lifting his chin toward the window. 'Him, Dale and that townie, Toledo. Said they were going to Toledo's house to hide out until the shooting died down. Left me behind to hold the fort. You got me through the door, Tate. Can you men help me — my chest hurts bad, real bad.'

237

Barrett Tate had little sympathy for the outlaw who had been trying to kill him minutes ago.

'Take a deep breath and try to bleed slowly,' Tate said.

Frost was already at the window, leaning out to look below at the deserted alley. 'There's a fire ladder nailed to the side of the building,' he said.

'You know this town,' Rome said urgently, tugging at Frost's shirtsleeve. 'Where is Toledo's house?'

'Two miles out of town down Creek Road. That's a hell of a walk.'

'You don't think they had horses outside?'

'We would have seen them when we rode past. No,' Frost shook his head, 'they're afoot.'

Tate nudged Gere with his boot toe. 'Stay awake, Gere! Look, are you sure that they said they were going to Toledo's house?'

'That's what Toledo told Mansir. I can tell you exactly what he said — 'I've got a little place just out of town. No one will ever think of looking for us there.''

A little place just out of town. No, Frost was thinking, Toledo did not have one — but there was such a place. His niece lived in it.

Clara Finch's cottage!

13

'Are there horses there — at the girl's cabin?' Tate asked. He and Frost rode side by side as they moved away from the battleground which was Climax on this night. Behind them were Rome and Calvin Weaver, who seemed more determined than any of them to track down Charles Mansir.

'No. Clara doesn't keep any,' Giles Frost replied.

'That's a break for us, then,' Deputy Tate said. 'They haven't a chance of outrunning us if they decide to make a break for it.'

'We'll still have to dig them out,' Rome declared. 'There's no way Mansir is going to surrender.'

'And they have a hostage,' Calvin said, touching the nerve that Frost did not want to think about.

Yes, they had Clara.

'But you say Toledo is her uncle, Giles. Surely he wouldn't want her put at any risk.'

'That's just what he's already done,' Frost muttered. 'Taking a man like Mansir to her house, knowing that someone could be pursuing them.' Maybe, Frost considered, Toledo didn't care about Clara's safety one way or the other, but only profit.

'He wouldn't have had much choice,' Calvin Weaver said gently, having correctly read Frost's expression. 'Mansir undoubtedly had Toledo at gunpoint, demanding a place to hide out.'

'I suppose you're right,' Frost muttered unhappily. At the moment he didn't care what had motivated the saloon-keeper to do what he had done. His only concern was Clara.

'With them on foot,' Rome said, 'it's a wonder that we haven't caught up with them already.'

But it had taken them all some time to catch up their horses. Frost's buckskin was standing and ready at the back of the saloon, as was Tate's dun. Rome and Calvin had left their horses tethered at the hitch rail in front of the Alhambra when they entered the saloon. Lando's horse had been available — he would not be needing it for a while, but finding another mount was more of a problem. They couldn't go out into the salvos of shots sounding up and down Main Street to look for one.

Calvin Weaver had spoken to the two Liberty Bell men who were still watching the prisoners near the outside staircase. Although neither of them wished to be left without a horse under the circumstances, Calvin as part-owner of the ranch had promised three horses from his own stable for the use of one on this night. One of the men had relented and handed over the reins to his strapping red roan, gambling that tomorrow would find him a wealthy man.

If he lived that long.

For now the small group of men walked their horses slowly through the

242

star shadows of the night along the trail where oak trees grew in profusion toward Clara Finch's tiny cottage. They had given up speaking, not knowing where their prey might be concealed. Frost abruptly threw up a hand and halted his horse. Through the woods he had seen the cottage, lights inside shining through its small windows.

'That's it,' he told the others, pointing that way.

'We'd better approach silently,' Tate said. 'Should we picket the horses?'

Frost said, 'I think so, and out here is good. No one will be able to find them quickly — and we don't want one of them riding off.'

With their horses tethered among the trees the four men started down the low hill slope toward the quiet-appearing cabin. What was really going on inside? Frost wondered. Mansir would certainly be ranting over the way the night had turned. From where they were the uproar of the pitched battle for the town of Climax could be heard faintly.

And Mansir would know that Tate was still looking for him on that murder charge out of Winona; his kingdom was very rapidly falling to pieces. Dale, Mansir's tall lieutenant whom Frost had met at the roadblock, would likely be posted somewhere as a lookout, watching from a window or from among the trees for approaching trouble. Giles did not know Toledo well even after his years in Climax. Would the saloon-keeper be wringing his hands, bearing the brunt of Mansir's fury, cringing in silent desperation?

And Clara . . . would she have been locked away in a closet or injured? Giles was pretty sure that under the present circumstances the last thought in anyone's mind would be to molest her, but the shock of having her home invaded by the notorious outlaw accompanied by her uncle Toledo would surely have been devastating. No, it was likely that Clara was safe for the time being. Unless Mansir decided that a hostage might help him to escape.

As they approached the cabin where a silhouette could be seen moving behind the front window shade, Tate motioned everyone to get down. From his knee, Giles Frost studied the area as carefully as he could in the darkness, but saw no one.

'If Dale is still with them, he must be inside as well,' Giles whispered to Tate.

'All right,' Rome said. 'What are we going to do, then? I say we just rush the house. We outnumber them.'

Tate pondered matters for a moment. 'This time, General, you may be right,' he said to Rome. 'Unless . . . is there a back door, Frost?'

'That's the only one. There's one more small window in the back kitchen, but that's it. The place is as small inside as it looks to be.'

'Can a man fit through the kitchen window?' Tate wanted to know.

'Not without great difficulty,' Frost said, pondering the question.

'Nevertheless . . . Calvin, will you see if you can circle the shed and come up behind where you can watch that back window for us?' Calvin Weaver nodded and headed off through the shadows in that direction, moving silently for such a big man who was wearing western boots.

'We have to break in the front door; the shooting will be immediate. Is there any way we can gain the advantage?' Rome wondered out loud.

'I can only think of one way, and it's very dangerous.' His eyes settled on Frost. 'This is your girlfriend's house, isn't it? I remember you and Clara were pretty cosy.'

'We were never 'cosy',' Frost snapped.

'But you are known there. It wouldn't be completely out of character for you to go up to the door and call out for her. There was a lot of trouble in town, and you just want to make sure that she's all right.'

'I'd probably get dropped on the porch,' Frost answered.

'Why? Mansir would likely ask Toledo who you are and maybe send Clara to the door to reassure you.'

'You're taking a hell of a risk with my life,' Frost said sourly.

'Yes, but it might work. Right now you're taking a hell of a risk with your girlfriend's life, the longer you leave her in there.'

Frost didn't take the time to argue that Clara was far from being his girlfriend. He could see Tate's logic, even if he didn't agree with him. It probably had a better chance of working than having three men just try to storm the door. Frost shrugged. What did he care anymore? He had been on the edge of death for many days now.

There were really few options. It was up to them. No one from the Liberty Bell soldiers in town could ride to their aid, not knowing the cottage even existed. 'All right,' Frost said grudgingly. 'I'll give it a try.' He unpinned the deputy's badge from his shirt and jammed it into the pocket of his blue jeans.

'We'll be behind you,' Tate told him. 'As close as we can get without being seen. If you have a chance to slam that door open, take it!'

'Assuming I make it that far,' Giles said, rising to his feet.

Tate slapped him lightly on the back. 'Good man. Don't forget that you're doing this for your girl.'

Giles Frost's answer was a grunt of disgust. 'I'm doing this for the badge,' he said, even knowing as he walked away that it was not for some tin star that he was launching himself into a certain exchange of gunfire. He only wanted to get near enough to the front door of Clara's cottage to give the plan a chance of working before he was gunned down.

Easing from the shadows of the oak grove, he strode quickly across the bare ground before the cottage. No one fired at him, but he saw the front window shade being opened a bare inch by the muzzle of a Winchester. His chest was tight, his breathing labored, but

— thankfully — no sudden bolt of electricity, no blinding flash from his headaches struck him.

The door to the tiny house remained closed, the shade drawn. For all anyone unknowing would have been able to determine, the remote desert cottage was still, its inhabitants going about their nightly routine.

Frost stepped boldly up onto the front porch. To have done otherwise might be viewed as suspicious. He rapped loudly on the door and heard a muttered word or two from within. One of these was 'easy'. He hoped that meant that the intruders were going to try to play this safe. Frost lifted his hand to knock again, but before knuckles touched wood the door was swung open. Bare inches as he was observed, and then a foot or so. He peered beyond the man opening the door, but saw no one else in the room.

'Mr Toledo!' Frost said with feigned relief. 'I'm glad to see you. Is Clara here? Is she all right?'

'Yes, of course,' Toledo said, though his expression was stiff, his lower lip trembling slightly.

'I'm just back from Bisbee,' Frost said, listening for the soft approach of boots from behind him. 'What is happening in town? There were groups of men fighting all up and down Main Street. Most of it seemed to be centered near the Alhambra. I was afraid that Clara might have been working there tonight.'

'No, no,' Toledo responded with his best attempt at placation. 'She's here; she's fine. She's in the kitchen preparing our supper.'

'That's a relief,' Frost said. 'May I see her for a minute?'

The question brought obvious concern to Toledo. His eyes squinted up on him, his mouth tightened. 'I told you, she's very busy right now,' Toledo said, fumbling for an answer to what would normally be an ordinary enough request. Frost heard, faintly, someone shuffling his feet inside, as if the wearer of those boots were growing impatient.

Finally Toledo, wavering, said, 'I'll ask her to step out for a moment. Please wait outside.'

'Of course,' Frost said amiably.

Frost waited, his rifle butt resting against the wooden planks of the porch. From somewhere — perhaps behind the black leather couch — he heard a small scrabbling sound as if a mouse had gotten in. It was no mouse. He thought now that he knew where both of the two intruders were hiding: one behind the leather sofa, one in Clara's room, listening from behind the closed door.

Clara was escorted from the kitchen by her uncle Toledo. She wore no apron, nor were her hands dusted with flour or any other substance to indicate she had been cooking. The unhelpful girl smiled wanly and took a step into the room, saying too loudly, 'Why, it's Marshal Frost! Welcome, Marshal!'

That did it. Dale, still wearing his leather chaps, popped up from behind the couch and fired two shots wildly in

Frost's direction. One whined off the door frame, showering splinters on Frost, the other whipped past him, losing itself in the empty night.

Frost drew and fired as Clara ducked into the kitchen and Toledo stood shaking like a confused, anguished soul awaiting his meeting with Lucifer. Both of Frost's bullets tagged the tall outlaw, one piercing his body beneath his left collarbone, the other slamming through flesh and bone directly into his heart.

Dale made a sort of confused gurgling sound in his throat and then fell to the floor, dead. There was movement to Frost's left and to his right. He went down, rolling toward Clara, who had held her position beside Toledo, who stood with his hands up, quivering, ashen-faced. Frost saw a man he had not seen before, but recognized from descriptions, emerge from Clara's bedroom with a shotgun in his hand.

Charles Mansir was bulky, not tall. His dark hair had been pomaded back; now it was in wild disarray. His small dark eyes peered into the room beneath an extraordinarily bulging forehead. A ridiculous brush mustache decorated his upper lip. He was angry and frantic. This was his last chance to live and he knew it.

Frost stretched out a hand and caught Clara in the back of her legs; she sat down hard on the wooden floor, skirt flying, as Mansir cut loose with his twelve-gauge. He was not able to attempt any more deadly mischief.

Tate and Rome Fletcher had raced toward the house at the first gunshot. Now as they burst through the doorway, quickly assessing the situation, both men whirled and fired off-handedly at the stocky Mansir, who took two bullets in his chest, grunted, dropped the still-smoking shotgun he held and slumped to the floor.

'That's a shame,' Barrett Tate said as he stood over the dead man, still holding his .44 in his hand. 'The sheriff had his heart set on seeing Mansir hanged.'

'Anyone else around?' Tate asked

Frost, who sat on the floor beside a flustered Clara Finch.

'You didn't have to knock me down!' they all heard her protest. Frost gathered himself with a sigh, rose and stuck out a hand to assist Clara. She ignored the gesture and struggled to her feet. Calvin Weaver had returned from his look-out post. Eyeing the room where gunsmoke still drifted, he asked Tate:

'Is it over?'

'For those two. I don't know how it's going in town.'

'There's not a lot of shooting from over that way,' Calvin said.

'Maybe it's done then — one way or the other.' Tate looked at Toledo, who still stood quaking, his hand thrust into the air. 'For God's sake, man, you can lower your hands now.'

Toledo did drop his arms, then began babbling to his niece. 'I didn't have a choice, Clara. We were going to get shot to pieces. This was all I could think of doing. I didn't mean to bring any harm to you . . . '

'I accept your apology,' Clara said easily. She touched her uncle's coat sleeve, glowered at Giles Frost and walked toward the kitchen, rubbing her rump. 'I'm making coffee if you men have time to stay for a cup. Meanwhile — *Marshal* — if you could drag those dead men out of my house, I'd appreciate it.'

Tate snorted a laugh. 'I knew she was stuck on you, Giles.' Giles stood staring in the direction of the kitchen, his expression one of disbelief. Uncle Toledo she forgave easily. Giles, who had been only trying to save her life, deserved nothing but her scorn.

Calvin Weaver volunteered, 'Come on, Frost, I'll help you move these men.'

They dragged the dead men out by their ankles. It took both of them to move Mansir. From the side of the house where they left the bodies to await morning burial, they listened to the night, looked up into the starry skies, breathing the fresh air in gratefully.

'It's over in Climax,' Calvin said, nodding. He added with some certainty,

'I'm pretty sure we won. What chance did a disorganized, unsuspecting mob of half-drunken men have? There'll be a lot of stories about how the Liberty Bell men beat back an army of real-live out-laws to be told in the bunkhouse.'

'There will be a few who won't be there to enjoy the tales,' Frost said.

'I know,' Calvin agreed. 'Let's just be happy that this wasn't our day to go. You didn't even get nicked in the fighting, did you, Frost?'

'I suppose Providence decided that I had taken enough lead in the past days. If that didn't kill me, it let me be on this night.'

'Coffee's ready!' Clara called out through the open kitchen window. Both men looked that way.

'That's your girl, huh?' Calvin said, as they walked back toward the front door of the cottage. 'Well, I guess you are a lucky man all around, Giles Frost.'

14

Giles Frost rose from his cot in the office of the Climax town marshal, rubbed his eyes and rose stiffly. He crossed to the front door, which he swung wide. The morning sun had risen not long ago and the desert was briefly tinted red. The far mountain peaks were gilded at their crests. Tugging his hat lower, repositioning his gunbelt a little, he went out to face the day.

The town was not yet awake, although the Alhambra Saloon had opened its doors for the usual bunch of morning drinkers. These old desert rats had resurfaced from their hiding places as soon as the outlaws had been driven from town. As had some of the more solid citizens, such as Johnstone, the banker, who had been hiding out in his home with a strongbox full of the town's money. Luke Waylon had returned from parts unknown to reopen his feed and grain store as had Waxy Loomis, who had lost half-a-dozen horses from his stable during the uproar. Each of these men felt that none of this would have happened if Climax hadn't let its marshal go.

Frost doubted that, but of course he allowed the talk to go on without complaint. Toledo was now insistent that they needed Giles Frost back, and Mayor Applewhite and the others on the town council agreed.

And so Frost was back, rehired with an extra five dollars a month thrown in. Life was good. All right he was lazy, would remain lazy, but he was perfectly suited to this job and planned to stick with it until the town rotted to the ground or blew away.

Giles walked past the Alhambra where Mayor Applewhite and Toledo waved at him cheerfully and a few early drinkers raised a toast to the marshal. He passed the early-rising Otis Johnstone along the boardwalk. The banker was headed for the Genesis Restaurant to get his breakfast. They walked along side by side for a few minutes. Giles assured the man that he would now be redepositing his saved money in Johnstone's bank.

The banker's thanks for saving the town were so effusive that Giles began to tire of hearing it and didn't mind separating from the round little man at the restaurant's front door. One of the waitresses, Irene, glanced out the side window as Frost passed by and offered him a harried smile. Things had not quite yet gotten back to normal. There were still a lot of nervous people in town.

Their lives had pretty much been shattered. Looking the town over by the morning sun, Frost saw little evidence of the siege of Climax. There was a lot more litter around, especially in back of the Alhambra where a large pile of broken bottles and broken furniture had built up. Too bad, but Uncle Toledo had wanted to build his clientele; the result was just not what he had hoped for. Otherwise the town showed few scars. Oh, there were bullet holes pocking the sides of the buildings here and there, but otherwise it looked much as it always had. Perhaps that was because there had never been much to the town that time, the desert winds and harsh winter rains had not already destroyed.

Giles's passing behind Luke Waylon's feed barn started the little brown and white terrier that Luke kept to begin barking shrilly, repetitively. Frost smiled. Things were gradually returning to normal. The terrier had never trusted him, for some unknown dog reason.

Waxy Loomis's stable was the next building along the alley. The back doors were open and Frost peered in. Waxy was shoveling out one of the stalls, muttering to himself.

'Hello, Waxy,' Frost called. The old man halted his shoveling and glared in Frost's direction.

'Just look what a mess they left me! With me not wanting to come into town for a few days . . . it just builds up if someone doesn't keep after it.'

'It sure seems to have,' Frost agreed. Waxy had a right to be in ill-temper, but then, Frost considered, the stable-man usually was in a foul mood even in the good times. Frost didn't enter the stable. There were small piles of horse manure everywhere, waiting to be taken away in a wheelbarrow. 'Maybe you ought to consider taking on a boy to help out around here,' Frost suggested.

'Maybe I would if I could afford to pay one, if I could find one to trust. Any boy growing up in Climax leaves town as soon as he's large enough to work, you know that.'

'Yes,' Frost answered, he guessed he did. There was no opportunity for a youngster in the forlorn little town of Climax.

'When is the town going to pay me for my missing stock?' Waxy asked petulantly. 'You know them outlaws made off with five, six of my ponies.'

Frost shrugged. He couldn't speak for the town council. 'I suppose they'll be considering your claim.'

'Considering!' Waxy exploded. 'Hell, it's all Mayor Applewhite's fault — all of them on the town council. If they hadn't been so stupid as to fire their town marshal — '

'They seemed to think they didn't need me around,' Frost said.

'You can bet they have a different idea about the matter now. You got hired on again, didn't you?'

'Yes, I did,' Frost said, tapping his badge.

'Well, I'm sure glad of it. I'll bet you can ask anyone in town and they'd say the same thing.'

That was the first friendly thing Frost could remember Waxy ever saying to him. He nodded his thanks and eased back out into the bright morning sunlight, feeling better about things in general, and himself in particular.

He started back along the cross alley where Dewey Skinner had fired at him, starting all of his problems.

And nearly walked into another gun.

Ada Weaver had a rifle in her hands and an evil glint in her blue eyes. She wore riding clothes — a divided buckskin skirt and a man's red-checked flannel shirt. Frost froze in his tracks, twenty feet from the girl.

'You ruined everything!' she shrilled at Frost. 'Everything was set up for us to take over the Liberty Bell once Calvin went east. I could sell that herd off at top-dollar prices to Charles Mansir, never needing to mount a trail drive again. It would have been a steady, very profitable income.'

'Unless Mansir decided to double-cross you and just take over the ranch.'

'You don't trust anyone, do you?' Ada hissed at him.

'Usually not murdering outlaws,' Frost answered.

'I only regret that the bullet I put in you up along Sabine Creek was an inch or so off.'

'I've always wondered who did that,' Frost said. He was looking for a way out, some place he could dive and roll to before she could fire her rifle. There was none. A shadow flickered against the ground and then a man followed it into the alley. It was Calvin Weaver.

'Put that rifle down, Ada,' Calvin said in a controlled voice from where he was standing behind his sister. Her head turned just a fraction of an inch as she held the rifle steadily on Frost.

'How did you know I would be here?' Ada asked.

'You took your rifle to the breakfast table and started talking. Maybe trying to build up your courage. You told Renee and scared her. She told me where you'd gone.'

'Calvin, this has to be done! He's ruined us. And now Father is dead!'

'He hasn't ruined us. Things are just the same as they always were. All Frost did was keep that maggot, Mansir, from taking over the Liberty Bell. There will be as much profit this year as there was last year after we drive the cattle to market. You'll have just as much as you had — isn't that enough, Ada?'

'And you'll still be there, running things,' she said.

'I'll still be there,' Calvin told her. 'I may go east to study sometime in the future, but right now with Father gone, it doesn't seem so urgent as getting those beeves to market.'

'We could have had a lot more,' Ada said.

'What more do we need, Ada?' Calvin asked, taking a step nearer his sister. 'Don't make me stop you the hard way. Put down the rifle and let's go home.'

Ada hesitated. Her finger was still on the trigger of the Winchester. At last, with an explosive sigh she threw her hands up and shouted, 'All right then, I will!'

Frost felt a shocking pain in his skull. There was a flash of blinding fire and he slumped to the ground, unsure if he would ever be able to rise again.

★　★　★

He awoke feeling quite normal but for the dull throb of a headache. Where was he? He looked around him carefully, not wanting to stir up the demons in his skull. Gradually he recognized the room — he was upstairs at the Alhambra, lying in a comfortable bed. Below him he could hear the hum and chatter of the saloon. He ran his hands over his body, searching for a bullet hole, but could find none.

'You're all right, Giles. You just fainted.' Glancing toward the source of the familiar voice, he saw Clara Finch, her needlepoint on her lap, watching him. 'Calvin Weaver told me all about it.'

'I didn't faint,' Frost objected.

'Yes, I know,' Clara said impatiently. 'I know that Ada Weaver tried to shoot your head off once and it's left you with a problem.'

'I think I'm slowly getting over that.' Frost swung his legs to the side of the bed and held his head in his hands for long minutes.

'Some people are getting tired of tending to you,' Clara said, placing her embroidery away in a basket on a side table.

'Yes, and I'm getting tired of a lot of things,' Frost muttered.

'Like me?' Clara said innocently.

'Yes,' Frost said, finding enough strength to rise to his feet. 'You, and the way you treat me.'

'I can't help it. I just don't like you, Giles Frost. What would you have me do, become a quiet little mouse of a woman who did your bidding cheerfully?'

'It would be a welcome change,' Frost said, looming over the girl. 'But then I wouldn't know who you were anymore.'

'You like me better this way, even though I don't like you?' Clara asked, keeping her eyes turned down towards her lap.

Frost held his silence for a long minute, and then said abruptly, 'You know what, Clara, we all have to make decisions.'

'And you've made one?'

'Yes,' Frost said roughly. He took hold of her arms and pulled her upright. 'I will have you and I mean to keep you. I no longer care if you like me or not.'

Clara struggled in his arms and he released her. He shrugged and looked away toward the window of the room, bright with new sunlight, and so he did not notice the little smile that now played across Clara Finch's lips.

THE END

We do hope that you have enjoyed reading this large print book.

Did you know that all of our titles are available for purchase?

We publish a wide range of high quality large print books including:
Romances, Mysteries, Classics
General Fiction
Non Fiction and Westerns

Special interest titles available in large print are:
The Little Oxford Dictionary
Music Book, Song Book
Hymn Book, Service Book

Also available from us courtesy of Oxford University Press:
Young Readers' Dictionary
(large print edition)
Young Readers' Thesaurus
(large print edition)

For further information or a free brochure, please contact us at:
Ulverscroft Large Print Books Ltd.,
The Green, Bradgate Road, Anstey,
Leicester, LE7 7FU, England.
Tel: (00 44) **0116 236 4325**
Fax: (00 44) **0116 234 0205**

Other titles in the
Linford Western Library:

Mr GUNN

Tyler Hatch

The members of the wagon train called him 'Mr Gunn'. A good name, and he'd earned it — but it wasn't his . . . That was the trouble: he didn't know *who* he was since he'd woken in a Union Army camp, wounded and wearing a dead man's tunic. Seeking out the widow of Captain Landis, the uniform's owner, Gunn finds no answers — only further questions. But when he is hounded as a Johnny Reb and falsely accused of murder, it's left to Beth Landis to mount a rescue mission . . .

SOUTH TO SONORA

Michael Stewart

After a ten-year prison term for killing a man he'd found molesting a girl, all Tom Jericho wants is a quiet life. But, the day before his release, the warden offers him a deal: if Tom infiltrates the notorious Crane gang and uncovers details of their plans, he'll be set up with enough money to buy a patch of land to farm. All he has to do is get himself arrested for murder — then spring his old friend Lee Crane from the prison train . . .

TOM RIDER'S RECKONING

Rob Hill

In prosperous El Cobarde, the respected sheriff Tom Rider is happily anticipating his retirement. But, barely hours after Tom hands over the reins of command, notorious local lawbreaker Jeb Deeds escapes from his prison train and storms the streets with dynamite, pursuing a vendetta against the eminent town founders. For a long-buried secret is about to emerge, and Deeds intends to bring a bloody reckoning to this town built on foundations of murder and treachery . . .

NIGHT OF THE GUNSLINGER

I. J. Parnham

With the town marshal laid up with a broken leg, Deputy Rick Cody must stand alone to protect New Town during a night of mayhem. At sunup Edison Dent will stand trial for Ogden Reed's murder — but Rick doubts his guilt. With only one night to uncover the truth, his task is made harder when the outlaw Hedley Beecher plots to free the prisoner. Meanwhile, Ogden's brother Logan vows to kill Edison and anyone who stands in his way . . .

HELL-BENT

Corba Sunman

Matt Logan, an undercover Texas Ranger, rides into the Texas cow town of Walnut Creek to end the local trouble. He expects it to be a routine chore of law enforcement; but from the moment of his arrival, events prove otherwise. Before he can even stable his horse, Logan finds himself forced to kill a man, and the shooting seems to set the tone for the job. For life is cheap in Walnut Creek — his own included . . .